NO SUBSTITUTE FOR LOVE

Although recently made redundant, nurse Holly Fraser decides to spend some of her savings on a Christmas coach tour in Scotland. When the tour reaches the Callender Hotel, several people mistake Holly for a Mrs MacEwan. Furthermore, Ian MacEwan arrives to take her to the Hall, convinced that she is his wife, Carol! Although Ian despises Carol for having deserted him and their two small children, two-year-old Lucy needs her mother. Holly stays to help the child, but finds herself in an impossible situation.

Books by Dina McCall
in the Linford Romance Library:

DINA McCALL

NO SUBSTITUTE FOR LOVE

Complete and Unabridged

LINFORD
Leicester

First published in Great Britain in 1986

First Linford Edition
published 2005

British Library CIP Data

McCall, Dina
 No substitute for love.—Large print ed.—
Linford romance library
 1. Mistaken identity—Fiction
 2. Broken homes—Fiction
 3. Love stories 4. Large type books
 I. Title
 823.9′14 [F]

 ISBN 1–84617–031–1

Published by
F. A. Thorpe (Publishing)
Anstey, Leicestershire

Set by Words & Graphics Ltd.
Anstey, Leicestershire
Printed and bound in Great Britain by
T. J. International Ltd., Padstow, Cornwall

This book is printed on acid-free paper

1

On that day — that very strange day — everything appeared normal until the yellow coach drew up outside the hotel.

Holly wriggled into a plastic mac, pulled the hood over her rebellious red-gold hair, and joined the rest of the passengers as they straggled out into the drizzle. This was how it had been every day of this Christmas tour of the Trossachs.

With her free hand she grabbed a bulging suitcase from a short fat woman. 'Into the dry, Mrs. Mills. I'll bring this.'

The woman relinquished her burden gratefully, and smiled up into Holly's face. She was not the only passenger who had developed a fondness for this resilient slip of a girl, whose friendly manner had done so much to dispel the gloom of a particularly wet December.

'It's not much fun for you, dear,' the woman commented, as they pushed their way through the hotel doors. 'You ought to be with people of your own age at Christmas.'

Holly tactfully refrained from answering. It was true, though, that this holiday had not lived up to her expectations — but anything was better than another drab Christmas spent alone in a bed-sit.

As the tour party queued in front of the reception desk, Holly looked around her, and felt comforted. The hotel was small, but cosy and cheerful. The gaudy red-patterned carpet and gold-striped wall-paper gave an air of warm comfort, and the streamers looping over their heads indicated that someone believed that Christmas was indeed a festive season. In one corner a large fir tree stretched out its branches. Not plastic ones, but the real thing — already shedding a carpet of needles, and festooned with coloured balls and tinsel. A smile touched the corners of her mouth. She could remember many such trees. They had one every year at the Orphanage. In later years, people would commiserate with her — but in reality she had not minded. After all, she had never known anything different, and the nuns had done their best to make it a happy time. It was only when she had grown old enough to leave the Home's sheltering walls, that she had known what loneliness really meant.

After that, there had been other trees, in the wards of the children's hospital where she had worked. Artificial ones, maybe, but no less exciting for the youngsters. She had usually been able to swap duties, so that she worked over the holiday period. There was never a shortage of nurses who had families they wanted to be with at such a time, and she had been content to share her Christmas with the patients. Holly sighed, a little wistfully. Even this chapter of her life was over now. St. Margarets had closed — its outdated buildings proving uneconomic — and its merger with the new hospital had meant redundancies all round.

So there she was. No family, no job, and not much money! But Holly was nothing, if not a survivor, and when she had picked up a brochure promising 'Yuletide with jolly companions. Travel through gorgeous scenery! Enjoy the hospitality of Bonnie Scotland!' she had, on impulse, dipped into her meagre savings and invested in a ticket.

'So you're back to visit us again, then?'

The voice broke into her reverie, and Holly came to with a jump, to realize that she had now reached the desk.

'I'm sorry!' she laughed in confusion. 'I was miles away.'

The man behind the desk looked at her speculatively. He pushed the register in front of her, and when she had signed it, took it back again, and read her name out aloud.

'Miss Holly Fraser! Well, well!' His eyes flickered to her face. For some reason Holly felt uncomfortable.

'Yes. May I have my key please?'

The man picked up a key, but held on to it. 'I was saying,' he repeated, 'so you're back then . . . *Miss Fraser*.'

Holly took the key. She had met men like him before. 'I could hardly be back,' she said sweetly, 'since I've never been here before!'

She picked up her case, and followed the others up the broad staircase. As she turned the corner of the stairs and looked back, she saw him still standing there, staring up at her.

★   ★   ★

Holly freshened up in her room. There was no point in unpacking, because the next day they would be moving to Killin, where they would spend the Christmas. The accommodation was comfortable enough, in an impersonal way — but she was used to rooms like that. You don't get much chance to stamp your individuality on an orphanage. From the window she could see over the roof tops to the hills beyond. The rain had stopped, and there were patches of blue sky. In the street the pavements were still wet, but there were shoppers bustling about. She looked at her watch. Lunch had been taken on the journey — so her time was her own until dinner. Sweet though her fellow travellers were, she had had quite enough of their company for one day.

She put on a dab of powder, pulling a face at herself in the mirror, as she noticed that she still had a few freckles, even though it was the middle of winter. Then she pulled on her mac once more — just in case — and picking up a shoulder bag, let herself out of her room, and ran down the stairs and out into the street.

Holly enjoyed window shopping. She had not expected that shops would be any different here from back home, but strangely enough there were things that stamped the place as 'foreign'. Meat pies, for instance. She was intrigued to find that they were flatter and paler than their English counterparts. Holly was quite an expert on meat pies. When studying as a nurse they had formed the greater part of her staple diet! Then too, there was the sound of the language — a soft Scottish lilt to voices as she caught snatches of conversation.

She took her time, buying a picture postcard to send to Felix. Felix, who had been left behind in London, much to his disgust.

'What on earth are you touring Scotland for?' he had exclaimed in horror. 'You'll get snowed in, or frozen to death. The food will be diabolical, and you'll hate it. Why not visit my parents with me? Mother would be tickled pink.'

Dear Felix! He was undeniably handsome, with his wavy blond hair and green eyes. Suave and amusing, he was no fool either, being a promising young surgeon, but, although Holly enjoyed his company, there was something missing — something she instinctively felt she would recognize when the real thing came along. For that reason she had deliberately kept their friendship light-hearted, and a visit to his parents might just possibly be misconstrued. So, on the whole, it had been better not to risk it until she was more sure of her feelings. All the same, she *did* miss him!

Thinking this, she bought some stamps at the Post Office, and it was after coming out of there that she noticed the toy shop. Its window was stacked with toys — monkeys that ran up sticks, model forts, soldiers that beat tin drums, and teddy bears.

She pushed open the door, and was charmed to hear a bell tinkle. Why not buy something for the Orphanage? She had, as usual, sent them a donation, but real presents would be nice too. Although too late for Christmas, there were always birthdays coming up. At last she chose a cuddly white lamb, and a Clansman, complete with kilt, who tossed a caber. That would cause quite a stir! She opened her bag, and fished out her purse. When she looked up, she was surprised to find the shop assistant staring at her, open-mouthed.

'I'd like to pay for these — if you don't mind,' she prompted.

'Oh . . . of course, Mrs. MacEwan!' The assistant flushed and began wrapping the toys. 'That will be — let me see — aye, thirteen pounds and ninety-eight pence. I'm . . . I'm sorry I was staring, but I was so surprised to see you, you see.'

Holly counted out some notes. 'I'm afraid you've made a mistake. I'm just a visitor, passing through.'

The woman stared. Then her lips closed in a thin disapproving line. 'Aye . . . well . . . you know your own business best, no doubt.' She handed Holly her change. 'I dare say the bairns will be glad of the toys, anyway.'

'I'm sure they will,' smiled Holly, and left — the door bell tinkling again, behind her.

Outside, she glanced up at the sky. The patch of blue had been short-lived, and heavy clouds were blending, giving the sky a leaden look. It was definitely getting colder. Holly clutched her parcels to her, and set off up the other side of the street, to the hotel. She hoped that the weather was not going to deteriorate. Of course it was a risk to be so far north at this time of the year. The travel brochure held a warning that the itinerary might be changed without prior notice — but since she did not really mind where she went, this had not bothered her. However, it would be nice if it stayed dry. The glimpse of hills and lochs had woken in her a desire to see more of the wild and mysterious countryside.

She was nearly back at the hotel, when she stopped in front of a shop to admire the plaids and tweed mixtures in the window. The tartans were bold and bright, providing a fine splash of colour, but the garments she liked best were the knitted suits in the soft heather shades of the hills.

'Be a devil!' she urged herself. 'After all — it *is* your birthday on Christmas Day.'

It was true. That was the date on her birth certificate, together with her mother's name — Maureen Fraser. But it was the nuns who had named her Holly, because of the season. The woman who had borne her — no more than a child herself — died that same night, without leaving any clue as to where she had come from. The mystery of her birth gave Holly ample scope for conjuring up all manner of forebears. She might — she thought as she entered the shop — even belong to this very area. After all, Fraser was a Scottish name.

'Why hello Mrs. MacEwan. Fancy seeing you!'

'That's the second time today that someone has thought they recognized me,' laughed Holly. 'I hope Mrs. MacEwan is somebody important!' She turned away from the surprised sales woman, and picked up a suit of muted blue green wool. 'May I try this?'

'Oh . . . oh, yes of course!' The woman showed her into a cubicle, and pulled the curtain across, but although hidden Holly had the uncomfortable feeling that eyes were still staring at her. It was certainly an odd situation! Here she was, in a strange town, being greeted by another woman's name! It made her feel uneasy, as though another personality was lurking behind her features. Not that it mattered. She would be gone in the morning.

The suit fitted her perfectly, and the soft colour set off her hazel eyes and fiery hair. The wool felt so fine and warm, that she could not resist its embrace. It would be just the thing, if the weather was turning chillier. Felix — she felt sure — would approve. He liked cuddly women, and in this she felt as cuddly as a kitten!

When she emerged from the cubicle she found the assistant in a talkative mood. 'You'll be just passing through?'

'Yes,' answered Holly. 'With Yuletide Tours.'

'Well — I hope you'll enjoy it — although it's a little risky at this time of the year.'

'It seems to be turning colder now,' said Holly. 'That's what made me decide to buy this.'

The woman wrapped the suit deftly, and slipped it into a carrier bag, bearing the name of the shop.

'Is it all right to pay by cheque?' asked Holly.

'Oh yes.' The assistant watched her make out the cheque, and compared the details against her banker's card.

'Holly Fraser? Will you be staying at the Callender Hotel?'

Holly raised her eyebrows. She had begun to feel that there was something more than professional small talk behind the assistant's curiosity. But maybe she was mistaken.

'Yes I am, though I'll be leaving in the morning.'

The woman made out a receipt. 'The laird doesn't know you're in town then?'

Holly stared. 'The laird?'

'Ian MacEwan, who else?' There was shrewd inquisitiveness in the eyes that looked into hers.

Holly found herself flushing. Obviously, in spite of her denials, she was still believed to be somebody else.

'I told you. I am *not* Mrs. MacEwan,' she said impatiently, 'and even if I was, I don't think I'd be discussing my business across a shop counter!'

She strode out of the shop, pulling the door to with a bang. Then she began to regret her outburst. She should not have reacted so strongly to what had probably only been friendly curiosity. She really should not be so impetuous. She had tried to cure herself of this trait, but there it was again! It was this business of someone looking like her that had rattled her. A good thing she was leaving tomorrow — it was positively uncanny!

Back at the hotel, she was pleased to find a girl at the desk who did not give her a second glance, and she was able to reach her room unmolested. She realized now that the man on reception at her arrival must also have mistaken her for this MacEwan woman, who seemingly looked so like her. Mrs. MacEwan! As Holly unwrapped her purchases, she wondered what her double's first name might be. Obviously she had a husband — a laird no less — and there seemed to be some children too. So this person, who looked so much like herself, was part of that magically complete circle that Holly had never known — a family.

As she re-wrapped the toys and packed them into her travelling-bag, Holly was still preoccupied. It was eerie to think of a mirror likeness of herself, leading a life of its own, quite oblivious to her — enjoying the companionship of husband and loved ones. She felt a pang of envy shoot through her. She had never been one to look backwards, but it was natural that she should hope one day to experience such a thing herself.

It was true that she had had many men friends — but perhaps the lack of a family background had made her too self-reliant, too afraid of being hurt, to place her heart into another's hands. Whatever it was, her relationships with the opposite sex always seemed to fade away before they became serious. Even with Felix she found herself drawing back. I'll end up an old maid, if I don't watch it! she thought with a grin. How often the nuns warned her that she was her own worst enemy.

'You are intractable, Holly Fraser.' She could just hear Sister Agatha saying it, and she could see herself as she was then, a sturdy unrepentant six-year-old, back from a disastrous weekend with would-be adoptive parents!

'You will never get placed with a family, if you won't try to please them. Why are you so difficult?'

How could she have explained that

she wanted to be loved for herself, with all her fun *and* her faults. Well — Sister Agatha had been proved right. She never had been accepted for adoption, even when less attractive children were. Her stubbornness had proved her undoing!

Holly gave a sudden shiver. All this thought of doubles was making her feel spooky — or was it that the temperature was still dropping? She took a peek out of the window. Daylight was fading. The street lights had come on, and there were less people about. Certainly the sky looked threatening. Perhaps now was as good a time as any to wear her new suit.

By the time she had taken a shower and dressed, she was feeling more her usual cheerful self. She brushed her hair vigorously, letting the crisp curls spring back against the neat shape of her head. Although she was not one to bother over much about her appearance, she was nevertheless pleased with the effect of her latest purchase. It was a pity that there would be nobody special to appreciate it! It *would* have been nice to have Felix with her. He was such fun, and knew just how to treat a girl to make her feel attractive.

She sat at the small bedside table, and took out her pen . . .

'My dear Felix. Having a wonderful time. Miss you very much. Wish you were here. Love, Holly.'

She read it through, and impulsively added three large kisses. She was licking a stamp, when the telephone on the table beside her began to ring. She hesitated — who could possibly be wanting to ring her here — then realizing that there was only one sure way of finding out, she lifted the receiver.

'Room Nineteen. Who is calling?'

'Mrs . . . er . . . Miss Fraser?' In spite of a certain urgency in the voice which emphasized the local accent, Holly recognized the voice of the man at the desk.

'Speaking,' she answered warily.

He rushed on, barely waiting for her to answer. 'I thought I should warn you. The laird is on his way up . . . I can assure you it was not us that told Mr. MacEwan of your whereabouts . . . we pride ourselves on being discreet . . . we don't want any trouble here . . . '

The voice rambled on half apologetic, half accusing.

Ian MacEwan — her double's husband? Holly felt a thrill of curiosity, tinged with apprehension. She was not sure that she wanted to come any closer to the lives of these people. There was clearly some trouble — but it was none of her business. Still — a husband would not be fooled by a superficial resemblance — and once he saw that she was not his wife, he would leave. She realized the voice was still chattering on, and cut it short.

'It's quite all right,' she said. 'I can deal with it.'

★ ★ ★

When the knock came at the door, Holly answered it.

'Mr. MacEwan? I'm sorry, but — as you can see — I'm not . . . '

The man pushed past her into the room, and stood glancing fiercely about him. Her first impression was of power. Power pent up in the vigorous strength of the tall body, power in the breadth of shoulders under the rough tweed jacket — but above all, power in the strong, even harsh, lines of the face dominated by craggy brows, and piercing blue eyes.

'Now look here!' she protested, as the door shut. 'You can't just barge in like that. You could at least have waited until you were asked . . . '

Her confidence waned, as she saw that he was not listening. His eyes were flickering over the room, as though searching and then he noticed the postcard to Felix. He snatched it up. Holly gave a cry of outrage.

'That's mine. How dare you! Look here, Mr. MacEwan . . . '

He read it, and flung it down with a contemptuous gesture. He looked at her directly for the first time. 'Can you not bring yourself even to use my first name any more?'

It was the first time he had spoken. His voice was deep and rich. Though cultured, there was enough in his way of putting words together to indicate his origins. He pointed a scornful finger at the card.

'Is that who you've been with for this past year? Felix — huh! What sort of a name is that?'

'A perfectly good one,' retorted Holly. 'Not that it's any of your business, Mr. MacEwan.'

'Ian!' He almost shouted the name at her. 'Dammit, woman, you've not been away so long that you've forgotten my name!'

Holly took a deep breath. 'Now — er — Ian,' she began soothingly, 'I can see you are upset, but if you would only look at me, you'd realize that . . . '

Once more she was cut short. He

crossed the room in three quick strides, and caught hold of her by her arms.

'What are you doing — coming here? Are you mad, thinking you could just walk back — after no word for twelve months! Did you think no-one would notice you? You with hair like that? Why did you go — for God's sake tell me?'

Holly was acutely conscious of his nearness — of the masculine scent of tweed and pipe tobacco, and of his fingers biting into her arms.

'Stop it! Stop it at once!' Her eyes were blazing up into his. She stamped her foot in a mixture of panic and anger. 'Will you let me go, and listen to me for a moment ... you ... you brute!'

His blue eyes snapped open in disbelief. She saw his firm lips tighten. He let his arms drop away from her. Then he turned, and sat down on the one chair in the room, folding his arms.

'There! Does that satisfy you? Now — I think you owe me some kind of explanation.'

Holly found she was trembling. Not that she was afraid — she was afraid of no man. But there was something about him that made her aware, in a way she had never experienced before, and it confused her. She looked at him nervously.

'Well . . . ' she began, trying to keep her voice steady. 'Now that we have both calmed down, I'd like to say that my name is Holly Fraser. I live in London — and I've never met you before in my life. If you'd stop for a moment, and take a good look you'd realize your mistake. I can see that your wife must have been very like me, but . . . '

She seemed fated never to finish a sentence. Her words tailed off, as he rose once more from his seat, and came towards her. Then he cupped one hand under her chin, and tilted her face towards his. As his eyes travelled her features, she stood conscious only of the warmth of his fingers on her skin, the depth of his eyes as he looked into hers, and the brown hair sweeping away from his temples.

Without warning he bent his head, and his mouth came down on hers questioningly, and then more violently. Holly could not breathe — could not think! Her senses reeled. As he released her, she realized with some confusion that she had not even struggled — it had happened so quickly. A flush rose up her neck and into her face.

'You . . . you shouldn't have done that!' she faltered.

He took a step away from her, and it was as though a shutter came down over his face. 'You needn't worry,' he said bitterly. 'It doesn't mean a thing any more. I was just making sure.'

He shook his head in an angry gesture. 'What are you playing at, Carol?' he asked. 'What do you think you'll get out of this silly game? Good grief, girl — do you think I don't know my own wife!'

2

Up till then Holly had thought the situation to be something she could put right with a few words. His kiss had made it much more dangerous! She realized now that she was alone with an angry man, who actually believed her to be the wife who had deserted him.

'This is ridiculous,' she stammered. Snatching up her handbag, she tipped its contents on to the bed. She picked out a letter, and thrust it under his nose.

'See — a letter addressed to me. And here's my bank book, and a library ticket with my name on it. What more do you need?'

He scooped up her belongings and tipped them back into her bag, clicking it shut. His glance was sardonic.

'That proves nothing, my dear — except that you have been using an assumed name. Now — stop this nonsense, and put on your coat.'

'Put on . . . oh no . . . oh no!' She backed away from him towards the phone. 'I'm not going anywhere with you. Please leave my room, or I shall call the manager.'

He looked at her standing there, a small defiant figure. As though reading her thoughts he gave a mocking laugh.

'Don't worry! I won't lay a finger on you. I need you at the Hall, but I'm not interested . . . not in that way!'

Holly found that hard to believe, her lips still burning from his kiss. 'Then why did you bother to come here to see me . . . I mean . . . to see your wife . . . at all?'

He turned, and stood staring out of the window. Something was making it difficult for him to find the right words. It was strange, the way she could read his feelings. His voice, when it came, was carefully measured.

'I accept that you never cared about me. But I shall never understand how you could walk out on the children. I can't forgive you for that. Bobby was old enough, at four, to ask questions. Little Lucy was only two. God knows what we would have done if Flora hadn't taken over.'

'Flora?' prompted Holly. She had become so engrossed in the unfolding drama, that she forgot her own accidental involvement. She knew only too well that women did indeed abandon their children, for a variety of reasons that were hard for others to comprehend. He swung around to face her.

'Aye — Flora! I know you never got on with her, but no sister could have been better. She had to do everything . . . especially after the accident.'

He stopped suddenly. 'As you didn't pay me the courtesy of leaving any address, I could hardly inform you.' His tone was bitter. 'About six months ago I'd brought the children into town. As we got out of the Land Rover Lucy caught sight of a dog, and ran out into the road. There was a car coming . . . '

Holly's imagination was quick to visualize the scene. Anything to do with children touched her deeply.

'She . . . she wasn't . . . '

He shook his head. 'For a while it was touch and go. But since then she has become withdrawn. Sometimes she won't respond at all — won't speak — won't eat — or even open her eyes.'

He glared at Holly. 'I can tell you, we've been worried sick — but a lot *you* would care!'

Holly ignored this, thinking only of the child. Her training made her aware that traumatic events coming close together could well make a small being want to withdraw from a cruel world.

'Don't the doctors give any explanation?'

He shrugged wearily. 'They say there's no brain damage. There was talk of sending her to a Home, though Doctor Sinclair says it's only shock. But I'm thinking she isn't so well in herself lately, and I wonder if maybe she's

sickening for something. Flora says not
— but I'd rather the doctor had a look
at her. Unfortunately he's away in the
hills at a confinement.'

He gave Holly a sombre look. 'Mrs.
Mackenzie came out of her shop as I
was passing, and was nothing loth to
tell me you were staying here.'

The woman from the wool shop!
thought Holly. I thought she was too
nosy by half! So that was how he had
traced her to this hotel . . . until now
she had not stopped to wonder how he
came to be there.

'What about asking another doctor?'
she asked.

'I'd rather not. I dare say Flora's
right, and it's nothing to make a fuss
about. I've left a message, and no doubt
Doctor Sinclair will come up later.'

All this time Holly had been
watching him. Here was a man used to
giving orders — a man with a dominant
personality. And yet she could sense a
cry for help, which his pride would
never let him voice aloud.

'I thought you had the right to know,' he said abruptly. 'She's your child, after all. You might want to see her.'

As ever, Holly's heart went out to a child in need. The very fact that she herself was so much like the child's mother made her feel somehow responsible. As a nurse she could at least see if there was any need to be concerned about the little girl's condition.

'Very well,' she said decisively, picking up her handbag and jacket. 'Though I'm not your wife, I'll come — but you must get me back here tonight, because my coach leaves in the morning.'

If she had expected any thanks, she was to be disappointed. 'I wouldn't dream of asking you to stay any longer,' he answered sarcastically. 'It is good of you to spare a few hours for your children.'

Holly sighed. His attitude was only to be expected, believing what he did — and she could not blame him. But at the moment she could see no way of convincing him of the truth. Once she returned to London she would send him a copy of her birth certificate. She would do that — if only to make him realize that he was no nearer knowing where his wife was, or who she was with.

And pretty silly he will feel then! she thought, as she followed him down the hotel stairs. As they reached the ground floor he took hold of her arm, but she shook him off.

'I'm not going to run away!' she flashed, annoyed because she could see the manager eyeing them knowingly. 'I shan't be in for dinner,' she explained at the desk. 'Will you please post this for me.' She handed him the postcard to Felix.

'Certainly, Madam.'

'*Miss!* Miss Fraser.' She corrected him crisply.

'A fine muddle you've got me into,' she scolded, as she let Ian MacEwan guide her to his vehicle in the car park. 'Goodness knows what the rest of my coach party will think.'

He opened the passenger door, and helped her in. He fastened the seat belt around her, and as he reached across she was uncomfortably aware of his face close to hers. Then he walked around to his side, climbed in, and slammed shut his own door.

'I couldn't care less!' He let in the clutch. 'You've brought it on yourself, Carol.'

'I'm *not* Carol! How many more times do I have to tell you, my name is Holly,' she insisted. She folded her arms, her chin tilted in what the nuns used to call her 'fighting' expression. 'You'd better call me that — because I won't answer to anything else!'

He glanced sideways at her. 'Play your little game. That was always the trouble with you. You played at being married, and you played at being a mother. Call yourself what you like. Call *me* what you like, for all I care.'

'Ian will do very well, thank you,' she answered demurely, pleased with her small victory.

They lapsed into silence. Through the darkening streets Ian drove in a relaxed manner, long lean fingers lightly holding the steering-wheel. Holly compared him with Felix. Women found Felix attractive, and yet to Holly he seemed a mere boy compared with this man. Age had nothing to do with it. She doubted if there was all that much difference between them. No — it was something about Ian's quiet air of authority, and his sheer masculinity. When she was with Felix she felt comfortably in charge — but there was nothing comfortable about being with Ian. This wife of his ... Carol ... how could she have left him? If he were mine, thought Holly dreamily, I would hang on to him for all I was worth!

She realized where her thoughts were leading her, and flushed, grateful for the darkness. It was ridiculous that a kiss — which was never meant for her in the first place — should trouble her so much. She gave an angry shake of her shoulders.

'Are you cold?' He broke the silence.

'Oh no — no thank you — I'm fine.'

He reached behind him, groped about, and then pulled forward a travelling-rug. 'Wrap this around you. The heater's on, but it's getting very cold out now. I think we're in for some bad weather.'

His tone brooked no argument, and Holly did as she was told, tucking the rug over her knees. She peered into the blackness. They were in the country now. She could see trees, and flakes of white appearing from nowhere in the glare of the headlights, and then vanishing just as quickly into the gloom.

'It's snowing!'

'Aye — it seems we may be in for a white Christmas.'

'You don't think it will stop the coach moving on tomorrow?' she asked anxiously. It would be the last straw, to get stuck in this place. The sooner she could put this incident behind her, the better.

'I doubt it,' he answered shortly. 'It's not lying yet.'

They swung away from the main highway, and began to climb. The road was narrow and winding. Snug in the enveloping warmth of the rug, and tired of staring into nothingness, Holly closed her eyes. Common sense told her that she was behaving rashly, but then she had often strayed away from the path of common sense. She had visions of herself as a child, skipping to a chant she had concocted from the words of Sister Agatha. 'Holly Fraser, you're im-pet-u-ous . . . Holly Fraser, you're im-pet-u-ous!'

Well — time had not cured her of that trait, but she did not think that she was in any danger from this man. Hurt and angry he may be, but he would not harm her, of that she felt quite certain. He would not deliberately hurt anyone.

Her head nodded, and she began to doze.

★　★　★

'Wake up. We're here.'

Holly woke with a jerk. They stopped, and Ian climbed out, letting in an icy blast. She struggled to free herself from the folds of the rug, and almost fell out of her door as he opened it. She gasped as she breathed in the cold air. Flakes of snow were still falling, she could feel them on her face, and there was a thin crisp layer beneath her feet.

'Come on. Let's get in, out of this.'

He hurried her to the door of an enormous house. She thought with regret that she would never see her surroundings clearly, for it would still be dark when she returned to the hotel. This was the strangest thing that had ever happened to her. She would have liked to be able to visualize it afterwards.

In the light and warmth of a wide hallway, Holly looked around her with interest. The walls were plain white, and hung with prints. There were faded but expensive rugs covering the wood block floor. On either side doorways led into rooms at whose use she could only guess, and directly ahead a wide carpeted staircase swept upwards. It turned at a small landing, where a deep arched window held a vase of dried flowers and leaves.

At first sight it was a pleasant house. A home where the smell of polish and wood smoke mingled with pipe tobacco. A home to be lived in, thought Holly — not to run away from!

Ian was taking her jacket, when one of the doors opened, and a stout comfortable woman came bustling in.

'Och, you're back then!' she began. 'I was wondering where you were at — you've been an almighty long time . . . oh!'

At the sight of Holly the smile faded from her well scrubbed face. She glanced in confusion at Ian, and back again at Holly.

'I never expected . . . welcome home, Ma'am.'

Holly cast a despairing glance at Ian,

who was busy ridding himself of his coat.

'The doctor was away up in the hills,' he said. He gave the woman a squeeze around her ample aproned waist. 'I left a message. Now, Maggie, we've not eaten yet — will there be something hot?'

She returned his glance with affection. 'There's a good stew, if that will do you. It will be ready in about a half-hour.' She looked questioningly at Holly. 'Will that be all right, Ma'am?'

'Oh yes. That would be lovely,' said Holly, but her eyes were on Ian. What a difference a smile made! All the sternness disappeared, and his eyes crinkled at the corners. Maggie obviously worshipped him. Holly felt sure he was a man who inspired loyalty . . . how strange that it had not been so with his wife!

'Come along,' he said. 'We'll go up to Lucy. Helen will be with her.'

'Helen?' she asked. It was difficult, the way he assumed she knew everyone.

This time, however, he explained that Helen was a nurse his sister Flora had engaged from an agency, to give Lucy the attention she needed.

'You should have told me,' accused Holly. Had she known a trained nurse was in attendance, she would never have come. It was not professional etiquette to interfere in someone else's case. Annoyed, she wondered if Ian had deliberately misled her. If so, to what end? Perhaps he was more devious than she had thought. Maybe she should revise her opinion of him. There may have been very good reasons for his wife's desertion!

At the top of the stairs, he led the way along a corridor, and opened a door. They entered a bedroom, brightly decorated with nursery characters. A uniformed woman jumped up, casting aside the luridly covered novel she had been reading.

'Ian — wherever have you been? You've not been bothering the doctor? I told Flora there was no need. There's nothing he can do, in a case like this.'

So this was the nurse. Holly took in the willowy figure and long legs, and the jaunty cap set on top of sleek raven hair. She noticed too the blood red finger nails — and wrinkled her nose with distaste as she smelt stale cigarette smoke.

The nurse had greeted Ian with familiarity, hanging on to his arm, and smiling up into his face with large, bold eyes, but now she eyed Holly with unfriendly curiosity.

'Helen . . . this is my wife.'

The shock on Helen's face was ludicrous. Her mouth dropped open. She turned furiously on Ian.

'You told me your wife had left for good!'

He shrugged. 'So she had — but now she's back to see Lucy.'

The look shot at Holly was one of pure malevolence. 'Really! Well, Ian dear . . . I'm afraid I can't allow that. I'm sorry, but it wouldn't do Lucy any good to be disturbed. As you can see she is asleep. I'm sorry . . . but I *am* in charge!'

And you'd like to be in charge of the whole household! thought Holly. It was not difficult to see where this woman's interests lay, and it was *not* in looking after a sick child! Her instant dislike for Helen made Holly determined to examine Lucy, after all.

'I only want a glance at her,' she explained.

'You've left it long enough, haven't you!' retorted Helen, furious at having her authority questioned. 'Your coming now will do more harm than good.'

Holly ignored her. '*You* asked me to come,' she pointed out to Ian. 'Well, now I'm here, and I suggest you both leave me alone with Lucy for a few minutes.'

Helen was about to object, but Ian put an arm around her.

'Come outside a moment,' he urged. 'I want to explain . . . '

As they disappeared, Holly wondered whether he was in love with Helen. It

41

would not be surprising — he was lonely, and she was certainly good-looking. A man on the rebound would be very easily taken in. No doubt he did not see the hardness beneath the glossy exterior, but if he did eventually make her his next wife, he would find out his mistake. Still — that was none of her business!

Holly turned to the little bed at the far end of the room. She gently pulled back the covers from the small form, and stood amazed. The tiny heart-shaped face, the tousled copper curls . . . she could have been looking at herself as a child!

But now was not the time to puzzle over such things. Murmuring soothing words, she laid her hand on the child's forehead, and felt the glands in her neck. Her practised hands told her that although there was indeed some slight infection, there was nothing seriously wrong. Lucy's temperature was only slightly above normal. As she continued her investigation, however, she began to frown. She noted Lucy's thin arms and legs. In her present condition she would have little resistance to any infection. Her skin was rough and dry, and she smelled sour, as though she had not been bathed for far too long.

Holly crooned gently to her, as she rolled Lucy on to her side. 'It's all right, baby. There's a good girl — just let me look at you.'

The child appeared to be asleep, her thumb firmly tucked into her mouth, but Holly knew that she was aware of all that was going on. 'We've got to get you well, sweetheart,' she murmured. 'It's Christmas! Christmas is a magic time . . . just you wait and see!'

Eventually she settled Lucy down, smoothing back the red curls, and kissing her gently on the brow. She stood for a moment, looking thoughtfully at the child's face, long eyelashes lying softly on pale cheeks. She made up her mind. Eyes snapping with indignation, she marched out of the room.

Ian and Helen were in the corridor, standing very close together. Helen was talking in a low emphatic voice, her hand resting intimately on his arm. As Holly approached they drew apart.

'I think you *should* get the doctor to examine Lucy — and the sooner the better,' said Holly bluntly.

'Why — what's wrong — is she worse?'

'Don't listen to her, Ian,' interrupted Helen with a sneer. 'Can't you see she's trying to cause trouble.' She turned on Holly. 'You should be ashamed of yourself, coming back where you're not wanted. Haven't you caused enough worry? You needn't think you can interfere over Lucy. I can look after her until she goes into a Home — that's where she needs to be, for specialized treatment.'

So that was her game — to get rid of the child, and have the father to herself!

'There's nothing wrong with Lucy that love won't cure,' Holly said icily. 'If anyone should be ashamed it is yourself.'

She turned to Ian. 'Lucy is not being looked after properly. I think you should let the doctor decide.'

'Well — here I am, my dears — what's all this about?'

A man had appeared around the corner of the stairs. Bluff and hearty, he looked like a farmer, with his hairy sports jacket and ruddy complexion. He greeted Holly with surprise, but made no further comment. He shook Ian's hand.

'I was up at the MacIntyres — delivering twin boys, no less!'

'Thank you for coming. I thought it best to ask you now, rather than having to call you out over the holiday.'

Helen gave a deprecating laugh. 'Really, Doctor! Mrs. MacEwan is a little hysterical. She doesn't understand Lucy's case. It's only a slight temperature the child has.'

'Well — let's see, shall we?'

They re-entered Lucy's room. Doctor

Sinclair spoke gently to her, and she allowed him to take her temperature, but still kept her eyes firmly closed, as though to blot out what was happening. Poor little thing! thought Holly. She longed to pick her up, and gently rock her fears away.

Doctor Sinclair checked the thermometer. 'Well, Ian — as the nurse says — it's only a slight temperature, but I'll leave you something to bring it down.'

Helen gave a triumphant glance. Holly moved forward.

'Doctor. While you're here, I would like you to examine Lucy's limbs — and her back.'

The doctor raised his eyebrows, but drew back the covers. As he examined the child, his lips tightened.

'How many hours a day has the bairn been lying in this bed?' he demanded of Helen. 'God, woman — she must have hardly moved since last I came. The muscles are beginning to waste, and she's developing bed sores. There's no need for this — no excuse at all!'

Helen went white. 'She won't get up!' she stammered, flashing a look of rage at Holly. 'She is very difficult to deal with . . . I've told Ian she needs to be in a special Home.'

'Nonsense!' said Doctor Sinclair bluntly. 'There is nothing physically or mentally wrong with the child. She has just withdrawn from an unbearable situation. She needs proper nursing care, and love. She needs stimulation. She shouldn't be allowed to lie here — or you *will* have trouble!'

Ian's face was dark. 'Thank you, Doctor — we didn't realize. I'll see things are changed.'

'I . . . I'm sorry Ian,' stammered Helen. 'Of course I'll do as the doctor says.'

Holly did not know why she felt so concerned — she only knew she could not bear to think of this little mite left in Helen's unfeeling hands.

'I think the nurse should be removed from this case.'

'And who asked you!' retorted Helen.

'Ian — are you going to let her speak to me like that — after the way she has behaved?'

'Mrs. MacEwan,' said Doctor Sinclair kindly, 'I'm afraid I would not be able to find you a replacement right away. You do realize it is Christmas.'

Holly made an involuntary gesture of helplessness. 'All right! I'll look after her myself.'

Helen gave a scornful laugh. Ian stared at Holly, a puzzled expression on his face.

'You aren't trained to nurse,' scoffed Helen. Holly was about to deny this hotly — but then she hesitated. Like everyone else the doctor supposed her to be Ian MacEwan's wife. If she insisted she was not, he might well judge her to be mentally unbalanced, and refuse to allow her to look after the child, and at all costs Holly was determined to get Lucy out of the clutches of Helen. She had one trump card up her sleeve.

She stared defiantly at Ian, as though

daring him to challenge her.

'Maybe — but, as you keep pointing out, I *am* Lucy's mother — and I don't want that woman in this house any longer!'

There was a stunned silence. Ian said slowly, 'In the circumstances, Helen, it might be as well if you left with Doctor Sinclair. No doubt your family will be glad to see you for Christmas. Would you like to telephone them first?'

Helen gave an angry cry, and flounced into the adjacent room, Ian following her. Doctor Sinclair looked at Holly.

'Well, my dear. Your little holiday seems to have done you good. You were very quick to diagnose what was wrong here.'

For a moment Holly was tempted to tell him everything, but she stopped herself. She would wait until Lucy had regained her strength. Then he could find another nurse, and she would be free to return to London. For now, there was no real reason why she should not stay. She had nobody to bother about her, except perhaps Felix! Nobody needed her, except this small scrap of humanity.

★ ★ ★

A little while later Doctor Sinclair left, and Holly was alone with her small charge. Little had she thought, a few hours ago, that by evening she would have entered another world! What had she let herself in for, stepping into another woman's shoes? What would Ian's attitude be now? She gave a little shiver. She could imagine he would be formidable when really aroused.

'Oh Sister Agatha!' she breathed. 'What have I done!'

She moved a chair closer to Lucy's bed. She would stay beside her until her temperature dropped. She looked down on the child. She was sleeping normally now, and the thumb had fallen from her lips. Holly touched her curly head.

Tomorrow, if she was well enough, she would shampoo those tangled locks.

Time went by, and nobody came near. Holly wondered what might be happening elsewhere in the house — what explanations — what recriminations. She was still deep in thought when Ian returned, carrying a tray.

'Your supper. I thought you'd prefer to have it here.'

Holly realized that she was starving. It was a long time since she had taken luncheon — a lifetime away, it seemed. He placed a table beside her, and she began to eat. The stew was thick, hot and delicious, and she tucked in with pleasure.

'Mmmmm. Tell Maggie it's gorgeous!'

He drew up another chair, and sat down. She glanced up, and saw those disconcerting eyes staring at her quizzically. They made her feel nervous.

'Are you mad at me?'

A smile touched his lips. 'You certainly surprised me.'

Holly waved a fork at him. 'I'm still

not your wife,' she warned him. 'I only told the doctor I was, for Lucy's sake.'

His eyebrows raised. 'So you're a liar too!'

Holly stopped eating. 'No, I am not!' she began indignantly. 'Well . . . yes . . . I suppose if you put it like that . . . I am, in a way.'

He leaned back in his chair, and folded his arms. 'But which was the lie, my dear,' he scoffed. 'When you said you were *not* my wife — or when you said you *were!*'

He rose to go. 'By the way, I've rung the hotel and asked them to send your luggage. In the meantime you'll find everything you need in the next room. Unless, of course, you'd like to re-occupy our matrimonial bed.'

Holly choked, before she realized he was mocking her. 'I've told Flora,' he continued. 'Naturally, she's none too pleased — after all, it was she who engaged Helen. Father is delighted though — he always did have a soft spot for you.'

Then he was gone. How many more people did she have to face? Holly was only beginning to see just what she had done!

After her meal, she explored the adjoining room. Someone had been busy, and there was no trace of the departed Helen. On the bed was laid out a blue silk nightdress with a matching *négligee* and slippers, and on the dressing-table was a brush and comb, and everything else she might require. Leading off this room was a small bathroom.

A little while later, and Holly had freshened up, and changed into the clothes which fitted her to perfection. Did they belong to his wife, she wondered — or to his sister, Flora?

She returned to Lucy's bedside, and turned off the main light, leaving a night light burning. There she spent the rest of the evening. At one time Maggie looked in and brought her a welcome mug of cocoa and some biscuits, but otherwise she was left in peace. It gave her plenty of time to think over the circumstances that had led her to this house. Was it just a strange coincidence — or was there some Fate which had brought her here at this particular time, so that she could help this child? Holly did not know. She only knew it seemed so like a dream, that there seemed nothing strange in sitting by the side of this little bed.

A couple of times Lucy stirred, and once Holly roused her to give her some medicine. Otherwise all was quiet. The evening wore on, and Holly became sleepy, and nodded off in the chair. It was about two o'clock in the morning when she checked Lucy's temperature, and found that the fever had broken, and it was back to normal. She gave a sigh of relief. With a yawn she turned to go to the room that was now hers. Then she stopped, her heart jumping, as the door began to open.

'Oh, you gave me a fright!' she gasped, as Ian crept in. He looked younger, in his pyjamas and dressing-gown, his brown hair all rumpled.

'How is she?'

'Fine. Her temperature's down. She'll be all right.'

He nodded, looking down at his daughter, a tender smile on his rugged features. Then he turned to Holly.

'Time you went to bed, then.'

Without any warning, he swung her off her feet, into his arms, and carried her into her bedroom. She lay cradled against him, gazing up at him with uncertain eyes. He bent his head until his lips were close to hers. She could feel his warm breath on her skin. Her heart began to pound — her lips tingle in anticipation of the kiss she knew was coming, but she lay still, unable to speak.

Then he dumped her unceremoni-ously onto the bed.

'Goodnight — sweet dreams,' he said cheerfully, and left — closing the door quietly behind him.

3

The next morning it took some time for Holly to remember where she was. In semi-darkness, her gaze travelled the room, taking in the unfamiliar furniture, the *négligee* lying across a chair, the open door into Lucy's room.

She yawned, and struggled out of bed. Lucy was sleeping peacefully, her temperature still normal. Holly returned to her own room, and snuggled thankfully between the sheets. She could afford a little longer in bed!

She was tired after her vigil of the night before, but now she was awake her mind was too active to allow her to sleep. Instead, she lay thinking about Ian's visit in the small hours. She had to admit that she found him exciting and attractive. In different circumstances he would be a man she could fall for. There was something about him

. . . something tougher, more dynamic, than other men. But, as things were, she dare not think along such lines. He was married. She must never allow herself to forget that.

When he looked at her, he was not seeing Holly Fraser. It was rather as if she was invisible. She could breath, and speak, and even fall in love — but it would not be her that he saw — only his wife.

She glanced through the open doorway, able to see the small mound that was the sleeping child. She would have plenty to do until Doctor Sinclair found someone to take over. She would be too busy to see much of Ian MacEwan. A little common sense! she told herself firmly, and everything will work out fine.

She rose, and washed, dressed and brushed her hair, wondering when her luggage would arrive. She must give Lucy a bath, and a woollen suit was not the ideal garment! She made her bed, turning the corners in true hospital fashion, and then ran water into the bath.

'Come along, sleepyhead! Time to wake up.'

There was no response from Lucy. Holly saw the comforting thumb was well and truly back in place. She rummaged through a chest of drawers, finding fresh clothing, and then bent over Lucy and lifted her. The child felt as light as a feather.

The bathroom was warm — obviously no lack of amenities here — and Lucy allowed herself to be undressed — her eyes still shut tight. But when Holly lowered her body into the water, those eyes snapped open — eyes startlingly as hazel as Holly's own! Two little arms gripped Holly like a vice. Two little legs scrabbled frantically, and Lucy let out a deafening roar.

'My word — so you *can* make a noise!' chuckled Holly, as she prised loose the clutching fingers. At last she had Lucy sitting in the bath. At first the child bawled lustily, but as Holly scooped the warm water over her, she relaxed, and the howls diminished into mere hiccups.

'How dare you! What do you think you're doing!'

Holly swivelled round. Ian's sister! she thought, seeing in the angular face and faded brown hair of the visitor an echo of his virile looks.

'You're frightening the life out of the child,' Flora snapped. 'She isn't well enough for this — you had no business . . . '

'There's nothing wrong with a good healthy yell,' Holly said firmly. She lifted Lucy out of the bath, and wrapped her in a towel. 'Lucy *needs* to let her feelings out. She has bottled them up for far too long. Look at her now!'

Lucy was on her lap, little pink feet sticking out from her wrappings. She was alert and bright-eyed, wriggling to look back at the water.

'If you really want to hear some noise,' said Holly. 'Get an earful of this!'

She leaned the child over the water, and began to shampoo her hair. Lucy responded with screams of rage, but soon Holly was towelling dry the rebellious curls, and Lucy was damp, warm and — thankfully — quiet.

Holly smiled at Flora, ignoring her outraged expression, and carried Lucy back into her room. Flora trailed behind her.

'Very well. I admit I was wrong over Helen. We assumed she knew best, and allowed her a free hand. That doesn't mean that *you* can walk back in here and take over. You have a nerve, after what you did! You broke Ian's heart — do you realize that? Having a good time, spending money, and running after men. That's all you ever cared about!'

Holly let the words flow over her, as she buttoned Lucy into a dressing-gown. 'Do you happen to have a hair drier handy?'

Flora gave an exclamation of impatience, her thin face flushing. She marched over to a cupboard, pulled out a drier, and handed it to Holly.

'You think you can come back here and worm your way into Lucy's affections. But you never bothered with the children before! Carol . . . are you listening to me?'

Holly sighed. 'Look, Flora. Surely Ian has explained? I am *not* Carol. I just happen to look very much like her. It's pure coincidence — a freak of nature!'

Flora sniffed. 'He said you'd tell me some nonsense like that — though he couldn't think what your game was. I can guess though. Oh yes! I can guess.'

Holly went on brushing Lucy's curls, now soft and shining. 'Then I wish you'd tell me,' she said mildly. Flora gave her an indignant look. Holly felt sorry for her. She wasn't a disagreeable woman. Just one who was worried. Things couldn't have been easy for her.

'If I really *was* Carol, what possible reason could I have for pretending I wasn't?' she asked.

'It's obvious. To hold up the divorce — that's what!'

'Divorce!'

Flora gave a triumphant smile. 'I thought that would shake you. It's quite obvious to me. For some reason you don't want one to go through yet. Go on — deny it! If Ian asked you to go tomorrow to your solicitor . . . would you?'

'I . . . I couldn't! I'm not his wife,' said Holly.

'Just as I thought!' crowed Flora. 'A fine excuse. All the same,' she added with a shrug, 'I'll put up with you for a while, for Lucy's sake. It'll be a good thing when Ian is rid of you, and free to make a new life for himself.'

Did she mean with Helen? wondered Holly, as Flora left. Was that why Ian had brought her here, thinking he would persuade his wife into a divorce? Holly wished she could prove her identity — but with the hospital closed there was no-one she could contact. She would just have to keep on repeating her story, until she convinced him. It was hard to believe that she and Carol could be so alike. Unless, of course, they were throw-backs to a common ancestor. She could try to find out if there were any Frasers in this area.

Holly looked at the child in her lap. At least she had managed to shock this small being out of her torpor, and that was the all-important thing. She carried Lucy to the dressing-table, so that she could see her reflection in the glass.

'Aren't you a pretty girl now?'

The picture was a charming one. Two heads, glowing curls touching. Two faces, so alike. Holly touched Lucy's nose.

'Freckles,' she said.

Lucy giggled. 'I is hungry.'

Holly hugged her. There was nothing much wrong with this little one! Perhaps if, after her accident, she had returned from hospital to her own mother, all might have been well. To have found herself in Helen's charge must have been the last straw. It was no wonder she felt deserted. Now — provided they were careful not to overtire her — she should make good progress.

They were interrupted by the arrival of Maggie, with breakfast, boiled egg with brown bread soldiers for Lucy, and for Holly steaming porridge, buttered toast and honey. Maggie beamed with pleasure at the sight of Lucy, and insisted on supervising her meal, so that Holly could have hers in peace. Holly warmed to her, charmed by the Highland lilt in her voice. A thoroughly nice woman, anyone could see that.

'Is . . . is Ian about this morning?' she asked casually.

'Och, the puir man has been out since crack o' dawn, checking the herd,' said Maggie. 'Have you no looked out of the window yet?'

Holly jumped up and pulled back the curtains. The sight made her cry out. 'Why! It's fairyland. Look Lucy!'

Outside, the world had turned to

white. The snow must have fallen heavily ever since her arrival at the Hall. She could see across a steep-sided valley, sheltered by tree-covered hills, now blanketed in snow. The sky was blue, and a pale sun made the trees sparkle. In a field near the house she could see shaggy-coated cattle, clustered close to a gate. The snow was trampled flat, and someone had been distributing fodder.

Maggie hoisted Lucy up, balancing her on her ample bosom. They laughed at her puzzled expression.

'I told you Christmas was magic!' said Holly.

'Your bag has arrived from the hotel,' said Maggie, as she returned Lucy to her breakfast. 'They sent it up with the postman, and he only got here by tractor. I doubt we'll be seeing anybody else the day.'

'Only one bag?' asked Holly in dismay.

'Why not go down and see — it's in the hall. I'd have brought it up, but I was carrying the tray. I can watch the lassie.'

So — breakfast over — Holly went downstairs, and there true enough was her overnight bag, but no sign of her two cases.

'Damn!' she said, and looked for a telephone. There was none in the hall, so she opened one of the doors. This led into a dining-room, dominated by a long polished table, and high-backed chairs. Above the fireplace hung a gilt-framed painting of a stag at bay. There was no phone here either so she moved on.

The next room turned out to be a library, but at the third try she struck lucky. Here chintz-covered sofas and chairs showed it to be the sitting-room. At the far end a log fire was blazing in a big open stone fireplace, and on a sheepskin rug in front of it sat a boy of about five years of age. He was building a complicated structure of bricks — a sturdy compact child, with a solemn engrossed air.

'Bobby?' said Holly, tentatively.

He looked up at her with eyes like his father's.

'Hello,' he said at last. 'Scuse me, but are you my Mummy?'

Her heart contracted with a pain that took her by surprise. What a question for a child to have to ask! It wasn't fair. Why did *she* have to feel guilty about it? When she spoke her voice was husky.

'I'm sorry, Bobby — I'm not your Mummy. I wish I was! My name is Holly, and I'm only here on a visit.'

He flashed a smile, and returned to his building. 'I only asked,' he said in a matter-of-fact voice, ''cos you look like her picture. I do remember her a little bit.' He frowned as he thought for a moment. 'I 'spect Father Christmas has sent you as a sub . . . sub . . . '

'Substitute?'

'Yes, that's it. I asked him, you know. Didn't I, Grandad?'

'You did that, laddie.'

Holly jumped. The voice came from a high chair facing the fire, its back to her. A head peered round it. A fine head with white hair and whiskers. A hand beckoned imperiously.

'So you're the lassie that looks like Carol! Come away in — we won't bite!'

Holly knelt on the rug beside Bobby. So this was Ian's father. She could see the family likeness, especially in the vivid blue of the eyes, and the strong bone structure of the face. Flora had borne a resemblance, but in the lined face of the old man was a kindly expression lacking in hers.

'Do you believe me then?' she asked. 'Nobody else does!'

He leaned forward, and poked the logs. A shower of sparks flew up the chimney.

'Let's say I've lived long enough to have an open mind!' His eyes twinkled. 'And how is the little one now?'

'Lucy? She's much better. Maggie's looking after her while I look for a telephone. My luggage has gone astray.'

He pointed across the room. 'Use that one, my dear. Come along Bobby

— let's go and see your sister — if we may.'

Holly assured him that a visit would be very much welcomed, and asked them to tell Maggie that she would not be away for long.

They left, the boy holding his grandfather's hand, and Holly began, for the first time, to realize what it felt like to belong to a family. These people, with the same blood running through the veins of different generations, had a sense of belonging she had never known. To her it was a precious thing — something she would so much like to be a part of. But how had it seemed to Carol? Had *she* found it a comfort, or had she perhaps felt a stranger here. Was that what had gone wrong?

However . . . it was all very well to philosophise, thought Holly. Her immediate problem was the lack of clothes!

She perched on the arm of a chair, and found the hotel number in the directory. Through the window she could see a terrace, with the dark smudge of footprints leading to a bird table. Beyond were the gardens, now hardly distinguishable, and further off the snow-covered woods and hills.

When she got through to the hotel she found that the coach had left early to beat the snow, taking with it her luggage. She was assured that it would be dropped off on the return trip. For now she would have to manage as best she could. She frowned. She did not have a great deal of money left, and there were things to consider, such as the rent of her room in London. Thinking about that led her to dial another number.

This time she spoke to her landlady, explaining that she might not be back for a few days. Luckily this delighted Mrs. Barnes. 'Nothing could be handier, ducks,' she told Holly. 'If it's all right with you, dear, my daughter and her hubby will stay there in the meantime. He's down looking for work. It would mean you needn't pay rent until you get back.'

'You're a darling,' exclaimed Holly. 'That would be fine. Yes . . . and I look forward to seeing you, too.'

With a satisfied smile she put down the phone. When she looked up she found Ian looking at her. He was still wearing a thick pullover and heavy boots, his face reddened by the cold.

'Couldn't you wait to speak to your lover?' he remarked sarcastically.

Holly flushed. 'I was phoning my landlady.'

'Landlady! So you're living in digs?' His tone was scathing. 'Is that why you've come running back? I couldn't see *you* living on a shoestring.'

Holly faced him. 'Ian MacEwan,' she said icily. 'You are the most pompous man I have ever had the misfortune to meet. I'm not surprised your wife left you!'

She marched out of the room, picking up her bag on the way, but he followed her, taking it from her hand.

'You've trouble over your luggage, I see,' he said, ignoring her outburst.

'Nothing to concern you,' she retorted. 'I can manage.'

'Stop bletherin' woman — you know damn well you've plenty of things here.'

He flung open a door opposite Lucy's room, almost dragging Holly through with him. She could see that this was his room. There was a four-poster bed, and substantial pine furniture, with heavy velvet curtains at the windows. The only real concession to modernity was a fitted wardrobe, which filled an entire wall. He slid back its doors.

'Everything as you left it. Not because I'm sentimental. I just couldn't bring myself to throw out clothes I'd paid good money for.' He pulled out drawer after drawer. 'Here — there's enough to last even you for years.'

'I couldn't . . . ' Holly faltered.

'Don't be so stupid. Take what you need. I'm going in to see Lucy.'

When he had gone Holly fingered the clothes enviously. There were more here than she had possessed in a lifetime, and good quality too, including a silver fox fur, and several evening dresses.

She was reluctant to use this other woman's clothes, but her common sense told her that for the time being she had no choice. She lifted out a couple of skirts and some blouses, a couple of plain linen dresses for daytime use, and some trousers, sweaters and underwear. She carried the clothes to her room, and put them away. Once she heard Ian saying goodbye to his daughter, she relieved Maggie, so that she could return to her kitchen.

Bobby was still in Lucy's room, and Holly amused the children by telling them stories, just as she had entertained the younger ones in the orphanage. It intrigued her to see the difference between the two of them. Lucy, like a small fire cracker, and Bobby old-fashioned for his years, and serious. It was a happy morning, and time went quickly by until lunch time, when Maggie returned to fetch Bobby.

'I'll bring a tray for you and Lucy, Ma'am,' she explained, 'but you'll no doubt wish to eat with the family in the evening.'

After lunch, Holly gave Lucy her medicine, and feeling that the child had had quite enough excitement for one day, popped her back into bed for a nap. A piece of sheepskin had been found for her to lie on, to ease her tender skin, and Lucy snuggled down, content to listen to Holly singing softly, as she changed into a pair of brown corduroy trousers and a Shetland jumper.

It was unsettling, and not altogether pleasant, to see herself in Carol's clothes. She wondered if she was in danger of slipping too easily into a life that did not belong to her.

She dismissed the thought as fanciful, and was debating whether or not to pop down to the library to find something to read, when Flora brought a message that Ian was waiting to see her downstairs. Flora had brought her knitting with her, and settled herself down, with a look that said that Holly need not think herself indispensable!

Down in the hall Holly found Ian helping Bobby into an anorak. 'We're going to cut a Christmas tree. Here — get yourself ready.'

He threw her a white anorak with a fur-lined hood, and dumped a pair of boots in front of her. Holly's lips tightened. If there was one thing she disliked, it was being ordered about. She had known too much of it in her young life. But there was Bobby, beaming at her as he pulled his boots on to the wrong feet, so she held her tongue.

She sorted him out, and then dressed in silence. She had got beyond being surprised at the way Carol's clothes fitted her to perfection.

Outside, the air was crisp, and the snow crunchy. It squeaked beneath their boots as they followed Ian to a small wooden gate, which he cleared of snow.

'We'll get a good fir from the plantation,' he said, pointing up the hill. 'You'd better follow where I tread, the snow has drifted here.'

Holly helped Bobby as he struggled manfully, his breath condensing in little white puffs.

'Dad, I need a sledge,' he panted. 'If I had a sledge you could pull me. My wellies aren't big enough.'

Ian stopped, and gave an amused look. 'You'd better ask Father Christmas.'

Holly gave him an enquiring glance, and he nodded in answer. They smiled at each other, united briefly in the knowledge that one small boy was going to be happy on Christmas morning. Taking Bobby by his arms, they swung him between them, bounding him across the snow in giant leaps. And in this way they climbed the hill to the point where the plantation began.

While Ian picked out a suitable tree, Holly looked back the way they had come. The house, nestled in the arms of the hills, smoke rising from its chimney. Down in the valley she could see the glint of a river. The air was clean, sweet and cold, and suddenly she felt a child again — but more carefree than she had ever been as a child. She scooped up a handful of snow, and threw it at Bobby, missing him wildly. He squealed with delight, and threw one back, and then his father joined in. Within seconds the air was full of flying snow, and the silence broken by yells and shrieks of laughter.

'Stop — stop!' spluttered Holly at last, as a snow-ball caught her full in the face.

'Sorry! I didn't know I was such a good shot!' Ian was laughing too, as he pulled off his gloves. He pushed back her hood, helping her to shake the snow from her hair. His hands were warm against her cold cheek, and as their eyes met his laughter faded. He stood silent, his fingers tracing the line of her face, down to the soft skin of her neck, his eyes greedily drinking in the picture her vivid colouring made against the backcloth of white.

Holly caught her breath. His touch had lit a fire in her blood. 'It . . . it's very beautiful here,' she said lamely.

He withdrew his hand abruptly. 'I thought you always found it dreary and boring!'

Her carefree mood shattered, Holly felt a lump come into her throat. It took but a word to bring the shadow of the past between them — and though the past was not hers, it seemed she had to bear the brunt of everyone's condemnation. She was tired of taking the blame for Carol.

She was glad when Ian began to cut down the tree. He stripped off his jacket, and she was aware of the breadth of his shoulders, and the grace of his muscular body as he swung the axe. He belonged to a very different world from hers, a world where a man had to use his strength as well as his brains in a struggle against the elements.

Soon they were ready to return to the house, but as they were about to start back Holly noticed a movement on the flank of the hill.

'Ian — what's that?'

She laid a restraining hand on his arm, and he looked in the direction she was pointing. 'Deer,' he answered. 'If we had my binoculars you'd see them more clearly. They're making their way nearer to the house, to take advantage of the food put out for the cattle.'

Holly stood enthralled. She had never before been so aware of the earth and the sky, and the living creatures around her, and her whole being responded.

On their way down, Holly dragged the tree behind her, while Ian carried Bobby on his shoulders. The return journey was certainly quicker than the struggle up the hill, and it was not long before they were back outside the house, stamping the snow off their boots.

'Run along in,' Ian told his son. 'I

want to trim these branches before I can bring the tree into the house.'

Bobby scampered indoors, and Holly started to follow him, but Ian blocked her way.

'Why *have* you come back?' he demanded fiercely. 'What do you want of me?'

Holly shook her head. 'Can't you try to believe me. I'm *not* your wife!'

From the look on his face she knew it was useless. She turned to leave him, and he shouted after her.

'Well, if you don't want *me* — do you want a divorce?'

She turned on the doorstep, and shouted back at him, her temper raised. 'I *can't* divorce you, if I'm not married to you! Don't be so . . . so pig-headed! Can't you realize that! You've made up your mind, and you won't admit you could make a mistake. Well — I can't help that. I'll be here until Doctor Sinclair finds a replacement, and then I'll be gone.'

She rushed into the house, slamming

the door, and there she found Bobby, still tugging at his boots. She helped him, sniffing.

'The cold does make your eyes cry,' he remarked wisely.

She agreed, and felt in the anorak pocket to see if it might hold a handkerchief, but her fingers closed around something else. It was an envelope. Inside it was a single sheet of paper. She read the first few words written there, and then hurriedly stuffed it back into her trouser pocket, and wiped her eyes on the back of her hand.

Later, safe in the privacy of her own room, Holly took out the note. She felt no compunction about reading it. It might hold a clue as to the whereabouts of the woman whose place she had taken. Holly had become a part of the mystery, even though unwillingly. It affected her life too, and she felt she had the right to find out as much as she could.

The note read ... 'Sweet darling

Carol. I'll be back on 28th. Meet me here at 2.30. Be sure — I beg of you, because there'll be no turning back. I want you for the rest of my life, but only if you won't regret what you are leaving behind.'

It was signed with a bold scrawl . . . 'Grant'.

The letter was dated on the 12th January, and the paper was embossed with the name of the Callender Hotel — the hotel where Holly herself had stayed. She slid the paper back into the envelope, and tucked it safely out of sight in her handbag. She sat deep in thought. So, this Carol *had* been sure of what she had been doing — it had been no spur of the moment decision. She had been sure enough to leave her home, her husband and her children, without a backward glance. Gone, without caring what became of them. That had been left for a stranger to do — and Holly had to admit it, she *did* care. Every moment she spent in this house involved her further in the lives of its occupants.

And . . . she had fallen in love with Ian MacEwan! She knew it. It was madness, but she could not help herself!

She wandered over to the window and looked out. She could not leave while the snow was so heavy. She could not avoid Ian while she was living in his house. She was caught in a trap. For Ian she did not exist — and for her his presence was a torment.

'Holly. Holly . . . I is hungry!'

Lucy was awake again, and demanding attention. Holly gave a little laugh. At least one could love children without feeling guilty!

'Coming, little one,' she called — and thrust her disturbing thoughts behind her.

4

Evening came, and Holly had to face the ordeal of a meal with the family. She changed into a Victorian-style blouse with full sleeves and a deep blue skirt which hung in graceful folds. She studied herself critically in the mirror. She would have changed her appearances in some way, to avoid the similarity to Carol MacEwan, which the clothes only served to heighten, but hers were not the kind of looks one could disguise. She tried brushing her hair away from her face, but it sprang back into its usual curls. In the end she gave up the attempt, and went to join the others.

The dining-room curtains had been drawn. A damask cloth covered the table, and a fire burned in the grate at the end of the room, its flames reflected in the heavy silver cutlery. Ian and his father were standing, their backs to the fire, deep in conversation. The old man greeted Holly, and pulled out a chair with old-fashioned courtesy. As Flora joined them, they took their places.

'You're looking bonny tonight,' said Ian's father. 'Don't you think so, Ian?'

Holly looked uncertainly across at Ian, but his lips twitched with amusement.

'I do, Father,' he said. 'The fresh air agrees with her.'

He smiled, and she felt a glow of warmth spread through her. Flora looked at them sourly, and Holly was relieved when the subject was dropped by Maggie bringing in the soup.

As a nourishing broth was followed by roast beef, the conversation turned to more general matters, and Holly let it flow over her, while enjoying the meal. There was nothing fancy about the traditional dishes offered, but the vegetables were fresh, the meat juicy and tender, and the roast potatoes crisp on the outside, and fluffy inside

— clearly Maggie was a cook worth her weight in gold.

Holly began to relax. She found the food, the warmth of the fire, and the hum of low Scottish voices, soothing. The room itself was solid and reassuring.

She watched the faces of her companions. The old man, ramrod straight, with his thick white hair and bushy beard, for all the world like an Old Testament prophet, and yet in a way more boyish than his son.

Then Ian himself, the angular planes of his face lit by the glow of a nearby lamp, as he leaned towards his father. His face was animated as he emphasized the point he was arguing.

And lastly, Flora. She could be attractive too, thought Holly, if only she would smile a little more. She must be in her early forties. Holly wondered whether there had ever been a boy friend.

The main course was followed by apple pie, with thick creamy custard, and Holly paid it all the respect it deserved. Although she was a competent cook, she seldom had the opportunity, or the inclination, to spend much time cooking for herself, though she occasionally prepared a meal for Felix.

She suddenly realized with a feeling of guilt that she had hardly given poor Felix a thought. She must ring him, as soon as he returned to his flat. She would have to explain why she would be away longer than expected. Knowing Felix, he would have plenty to say about it!

Holly became aware that the topic of conversation had changed. Ian's father was speaking.

'You'll not be having a party for Hogmanay this year, Ian?'

There was a silence which became uncomfortable. Holly looked up, and found all eyes on her. *Now* what am I supposed to have done? she thought.

Ian gave his father a vexed frown. 'No, Father. I don't think, in the circumstances, we'll bother this year.'

The old man persisted. 'But Malcolm will be coming, as usual, will he not?'

Ian's voice showed a trace of exasperation. 'Aye — he will if he can get through the snow that is. It was arranged weeks ago, as you well know.'

Flora jumped up. 'Do you want coffee Father? Ian? . . . Carol?'

She rattled the coffee cups, and from her obvious agitation Holly guessed that whoever Malcolm might be, his expected presence affected Flora far more than anyone else. But what had it to do with her? It was just another of the mysteries that surrounded the family. Holly made a resolve to have a long chat with Ian's father as soon as she found an opportunity. She felt sure he could answer many of her questions, if he would.

He saw her looking at him, and smiled. 'It will be a quiet Christmas for you, my dear.'

'I don't mind that,' she assured him.

'I'm not keen on parties — I never have been.'

There was another long hush, and again the accusing eyes. Holly felt her temper rising. She replaced her cup on its saucer. 'From the looks I'm getting,' she said, 'I take it that Ian's wife did not share my opinion. Well, if you think about it you'll realize that it is another proof that I'm *not* Carol. Now, if you'll excuse me, I really ought to check that Lucy is still asleep. By the way, Flora, in case you've forgotten, *my* name is Holly!'

As she closed the door behind her she could hear the old man's voice. 'I think the lassie's telling the truth, you know Ian — strange though it may seem.'

Flora's voice answered him. 'Father — don't be so foolish. You're always far too easily taken in. Can you not see it's all an act? She'll have her reasons for it, mark my words.'

Holly lingered for a moment, hoping to hear what Ian might say, but the voices were lowered, so she returned to her room, to spend the evening alone.

★　★　★

The following day was Christmas Eve. During the night more snow had fallen, and the sky threatened more to come. The morning followed the pattern of the previous day. Lucy's condition was satisfactory, but now that the novelty of Holly's arrival had worn off there was a tendency for her to withdraw again. Holly had been expecting this, and countered it by keeping her active. Bobby was a great help. He arrived during the morning, bringing with him a box full of toys and drawing materials, and showed great patience with his little sister. He would have liked to take her outside to play, but Holly explained she was not ready for that yet, though hopefully it would not be long before she could venture out of doors. As a move towards it Holly decided it was high time Lucy stopped living in her night clothes. Most of her dresses were too fancy for play, but Maggie managed to find a pair of dungarees and a jumper that Bobby had outgrown.

It gave Holly a great feeling of satisfaction to see the curly-headed little mite squatting on the floor beside Bobby. There was little fear of him overtiring Lucy. Although full of fun he was mature for his age, able to carry on an adult conversation one minute, and collapse into childish giggles the next.

Holly had always loved children, but these two were special. For some reason they had found an immediate home in her heart, and they in turn responded to her.

★   ★   ★

After lunch Flora took over, leaving Holly free for a few hours. Bobby wanted her to go gathering holly with him and his father, but she declined. She did not want another encounter with Ian just yet. She found his presence too disturbing, so when Bobby ran off she tracked down Ian's father, in the west wing.

He was delighted to see her. 'Come in, come in. Sit down and talk to an old man.'

He swept a heap of books from a chair, and dislodged a sleepy cat, who jumped onto a bureau and curled up on some papers. 'So you found me in my den,' he chuckled. He picked up a briar pipe and stuffed tobacco into it from a tin, pushing it into the bowl with his fingers.

'I have my own rooms,' he explained between puffs. 'I can be as untidy as I like here. Flora won't countenance it elsewhere.'

Holly smiled. She could understand Flora's reservations. The room was stacked with books. Trophies, silver cups and rosettes jostled for space on shelves. Photographs crowded the walls, and the top of an ancient piano, and two double-barrel shotguns hung on hooks above the door. The chairs were filled with oddments of all kinds. Holly noticed a teddy bear on one.

'Does Flora have her own rooms?'

'Aye — the east wing is hers, but we all come together for meals. The house was built by my grandfather. Thirteen children he had, and I was the only son of the eldest. I took the house and part of the land when my father died. It's a big place for Flora to look after, and only Maggie to help. Young girls don't want to go into service these days. They're off to the town to work in the shops.'

Holly examined the trophies. 'What were these awarded for — the cattle?'

'Aye — the herd. I began it, and Ian took it over from me. There isn't another like it. They're bred from a strain of Highland beasts that nearly died out — and would have, but for us. They're famous, you know. Ian has his hands full, especially when he's asked to lecture about them.'

He puffed again. 'Of course, Ian is the sort to get on. The herd is all that

93

matters to him. A cold and callous man, he is — and overbearing too — even though he is my own son. No doubt you've found that out by now.'

Holly looked at him in amazement. How could he speak of Ian in that way! She remembered the affection in Ian's eyes when he was with his father.

'You can't mean that!' she protested. 'Anyone can see that his family mean everything to him.' She struggled with the words. 'He's not domineering . . . just strong. And sensitive too. He's certainly not a cold man!'

The old man chuckled, and leaned forward to pat her knee. 'Now I know you're not Carol,' he said. 'Forgive me, but I had to be sure! Oh, you're alike as two peas, I'll grant you that. You're maybe a wee bit thinner, and your hair shorter, but these things can change over a year. What you can't change is the way you feel. Carol would have agreed with me, you see. That is how she felt.'

Holly's eyes filled with tears. It was

such a relief to hear him say this — to have someone really see her as herself. 'Why can't Ian and Flora see it too?' she asked. 'Surely Ian should know better than anyone that I'm not his wife.'

He gave a snort of amusement. 'Don't you believe it! Haven't you noticed that people see what they *expect* to see — or what they *want* to see? Ian and Flora are too involved — Ian particularly. What is a man to think when he finds a woman, the image of his wife, in the hotel she ran away from . . . eh? Especially when he's been hunting for her this past twelve months. It would be strange if he did *not* believe it to be her!'

'They say . . . you liked her.'

The old man tapped out his pipe. 'She was barely seventeen when she came here, and spoiled at that! I warned Ian, but he wouldn't listen. Oh, I was fond of her. She was pretty and bright. She brought life and colour with her, but she brought trouble too.'

Holly leaned forward. 'Tell me about her,' she begged. 'Tell me everything!'

★   ★   ★

It was in London, she learned to her surprise, that Carol and Ian had met. Ian fell head over heels in love. Carol was unlike any girl he had known, with her ready smile and elfin eyes. He could not take his eyes off her.

It was a whirlwind romance. Carol's parents were so overawed at the thought of their daughter marrying a laird that they gave their consent, in spite of her youth.

There had been a grand wedding, with swinging kilts and the swirl of bagpipes. At first, all had gone well, but before long Carol grew bored. She resented Ian's work, and the time he had to spend away from her. She had no experience of running a home, but thwarted Flora's attempts to instruct her. Ian taught her how to drive, and bought her a car, and she made frequent trips into town to buy clothes. He could deny her nothing.

As time went by, Ian wanted to start a family, but Carol had no intention of tying herself down. Then, in her unpredictable way, she changed her mind. Bobby arrived, and close after him, Lucy. Ian was overjoyed, but Carol showed no further interest in the children, and it was Flora who looked after them.

Ian constantly made allowances for his young wife. He took her out whenever he could, invited friends, and threw parties, but this caused more trouble.

Here Ian's father paused. Holly could see he was looking back, and even the memory of those events made him sad.

'What sort of trouble?'

He shook his head. 'It was as if . . . she had a devil in her. As if she was determined to wreck the marriage. The more patient Ian was, the worse she grew. She made up to the men — no matter who they were. It was an embarrassment to Ian's friends. Of course, some of them took advantage — but none of them escaped, not even Malcolm.'

'Malcolm? The man who's coming here tomorrow?'

He nodded. 'Flora's young man. Well, maybe not so young, but a good man — an accountant, who lives up along the top road. We were glad Flora had found her own happiness. They'd almost decided on a day for the wedding, but at the party on Hogmanay last, there was real trouble.'

'What happened?'

'Oh . . . I can guess, lassie — but I didn't hear the details. Children never tell their parents — have you noticed that? We protect them when they are little, and they try to protect us when we get old! Aye . . . well, whatever it was, there was a terrible row. A few weeks later Carol disappeared. We found her car in the hotel car park with a note. She left Ian for a man she'd been meeting for some weeks.'

Holly could see in his face the hurt he felt, not just because of his son's unhappiness, but because of the damage to the family. 'What about Carol's parents? Didn't she tell them where she went?'

He shook his head. 'They were terribly upset. They had a note to say she was safe, but that was all. I believe she was afraid Ian would bring her back — and she didn't want that.'

Holly sat in silence. Now she could understand better — understand Ian's need to find the wife he loved so much. This was what blinded him to the fact that she was not Carol. Did he still love her? she wondered.

A thought struck her. 'If Flora and Malcolm made up their quarrel,' she asked, 'why didn't they get married?'

He gave a wry smile. 'Duty! Flora's always been hot on duty. There were the children to consider, and the house to run. Ian tried to make her go, but she wouldn't hear of it. I believe she thought there might be a chance when that nurse came . . . '

'Couldn't Malcolm have come here? There's surely room?'

'No, no! Pride, don't you see. Malcolm wants his wife in his own home. Why should he live in somebody else's? A beautiful home it is, too. No — he is just waiting.'

'Poor Flora,' murmured Holly. Poor everyone! And yet, in a way she could understand it. Carol had been too young to be shut away up here, before she had even begun to live. What a mess for all of them!

She stayed for a while. Ian's father had many happier anecdotes. He told her of the days when oil lamps had been their only illumination, and paraffin their means of cooking. He told her about stalking the deer in the hills, and how he had been lost out there, when he was no older than Bobby. Holly was enthralled.

'You should write a book!'

His face lit up. 'Why, lassie — that's just what I'm trying to do, but it takes an uncommon long time!'

He indicated heaps of manuscripts, all written in beautiful copper-plate handwriting.

'I could help,' she said eagerly. 'I learned to type . . . and though I'm not very fast I could copy these for you, if you could find a machine. That is . . . if you'd like me to.'

'Are you sure?' He was as delighted as a child. 'I'll ask Ian. I believe he has a spare typewriter in his office. We could start once Christmas is over. But won't you be too busy?'

'I could do it in the afternoons, when Flora is with the children,' she explained. 'I believe Flora likes to have them to herself for a while.'

And it will keep me out of Ian's way! she thought.

'Holly! Grandad!' The door flew open and Bobby burst in. 'We're going to decorate the tree!' He tugged at Holly's hand. 'Dad says come and help. Grandad — are you coming?'

They followed him into the hallway,

where the tree had been set in a tub. Flora was there, with Lucy who looked bewildered, and Ian was there too, sorting out a string of coloured lights.

He pointed to a box of decorations. 'You can help the children put these on the tree, while we pin up the holly. Bobby and I picked a fine big bunch from behind the house.'

'Holly! We're going to pin you on the wall, with a red berry on top!' Bobby pointed to her red curls, and collapsed helpless with mirth.

'Aye — and she's got some prickles too,' said Ian drily. His eyes met hers. 'I like your choice of a new name. It suits you.'

Holly started sorting out the shining baubles. It was better not to answer him. He was spoiling for another fight, and though she could understand this now, she would not give him the satisfaction of seeing her rise to the bait. It was only by calmly ignoring his remarks that she would finally convince him.

Bobby, having recovered from his giggles, came to help her, Lucy hopping on one leg with excitement. Soon the two children were fixing the decorations to the spiky branches — red, blue and gold glass balls, coloured lanterns, and strands of silver tinsel. Ian's father hovered in the background, giving directions which nobody followed! Ian climbed up the ladder to pin the holly, and Flora helped him to fix the paper streamers.

'Dad — the tree's ready. Switch on the lights!' demanded Bobby.

Ian flicked the switch. The lights came on, and the tree sprang into life, twinkling with colour. Lucy gave a sigh, and clutched Holly's hand.

'It makes a pretty sight, sure enough!' Maggie had come to join them, wiping flour from her hands with her apron. 'I mind when Master Ian was but a laddie himself, dressing the tree. But where's the star? There was always a star.'

They looked around. 'Lucy!' cried Holly. Lucy had the tinselled star, trying to fix it on to her head.

'Give it to me, sweetheart,' said Flora. 'The wee star goes on the top of the tree.'

'I'll fix it up,' said Ian.

'No — it's all right,' said Flora. 'I'll do it.' She dragged the ladder nearer to the tree, and climbed up.

'Do be careful, lass,' urged her father.

'Do stop fussing, Father,' said Flora. She leaned over precariously. The ladder teetered.

'Flora — take care!' gasped Holly.

'Will you all stop telling me . . . oh!'

As she fell, Ian tried to catch her, but she slipped from his grasp and landed heavily, the ladder overturned on top of her, her left arm twisted awkwardly. Lucy set up a wail, frightened at the commotion.

'Ring the doctor, Ian — hurry now.'

'Father — you know nobody can get through — the road's shut.'

'Dad! Aunt Flora's not dead, is she?'

'Oh, the puir wee soul!'

Holly pushed her way through them,

and knelt beside Flora. She turned to the old man, seeing the anxiety in his face.

'Father, would you take the children to your room. Don't worry, Flora will be all right. Maggie — make a cup of tea will you — a sweet one for Flora please. She may be a little shocked.'

She examined a gash on Flora's forehead, and checked the pupils of her eyes. She straightened out Flora's arm. 'Ian — could you fetch some hot water and disinfectant, and any bandages you have . . . and a scarf or piece of material for a sling.'

As order prevailed Holly cleaned Flora's cut, and attended to her arm. Flora was conscious now, and they helped her into a chair, where Maggie held a cup of tea to her lips.

'I should have been more careful,' said Flora. 'I feel so stupid — giving you all a fright, and upsetting the bairns.'

'*And* your father,' smiled Holly. 'Ian — perhaps you could let him know everything is all right.' She turned to Flora. 'All the same you'll have to keep that arm in a sling for a few days.'

'Don't be silly,' said Flora. 'How can I? There's so much to do. Christmas Day tomorrow, and Malcolm coming. Maggie can't manage.'

'Dinna fret yourself,' scolded Maggie. 'I can manage fine!'

'You seem to forget I am here too,' said Holly. 'If you and Father keep an eye on the children, I can help Maggie in the kitchen. I promise you, Flora, it will be no trouble. Don't worry about a thing.'

★ ★ ★

The rest of the day was busy. Holly persuaded Flora to rest. She saw to the children's teas, and got them to bed. Stockings were produced, and hung at the end of the beds. Lucy was too young to realize what was happening, and went off to sleep easily enough, but Bobby became so overexcited that only a stern word from his father calmed him down.

Later that evening, Flora reluctantly accepted Holly's help in preparing for bed. 'I must say, you've been a great help,' she conceded.

'Have a good night's sleep,' said Holly gently. 'I'm afraid you'll feel very stiff in the morning.'

One more task had to be performed that evening. When the children were fast asleep Holly gathered up the stockings and took them to the sitting-room. Ian was alone, surrounded by odds and ends of stocking fillers. Holly sat beside him, and began to fill Lucy's stocking. A tangerine, tucked well into the toe, followed by chocolate money, a pair of new slippers, colouring book and crayons, and plasticine. Finally, a rag doll with long golden plaits and big blue eyes that bore a definite squint.

'Flora made that,' remarked Ian with a laugh.

'She'll love it!' said Holly. She

remembered the two gifts still packed in her bag. 'Ian — I have some presents for the children. When shall I give them?'

'As usual — when we give the things from under the tree, after dinner.' He took the stockings, now elongated and heavy, and moved them out of the way. He turned to face her.

'So that's the real reason for coming back! I knew you couldn't really have forgotten the children.'

'Ian . . . ' Holly wanted to stop him, to explain about the gifts for the orphanage, but as he took hold of her hands the words flew out of her head. He drew closer to her.

'Thank you for the way you coped today. I was wrong. You *have* grown up since you left. The way you took charge was magnificent.'

Now was the time to explain about her training . . . to make him realize.

'Ian,' she began again. 'I must tell you that in London I . . . '

'No!' He stopped her lips with his

fingers. His face was close to hers now, making her pulse race. 'I don't want to know what you did in London. You are here with me now, and I feel closer to you than I ever have before . . . don't spoil it!'

He drew her against him, and she closed her eyes. She knew she should insist on explaining. She could make some flippant remark to break the spell. She could get up and walk away. The choice was hers. But she did none of these things.

With a sigh of surrender she raised her face to his, and as his lips came down on hers, warm and gentle, her arms slid around his neck. His grip tightened, and as she felt passion rise within him, her own body responded. She gave herself up to the sweetness of his kiss. A kiss that seemed to go on and on for ever.

5

'Holly, Holly! Look what Father Christmas has brought me!'

Holly groaned, and reached out a hand to turn on the bedside lamp. She looked at Bobby, his pyjamas awry, brown hair standing on end.

'I know it's Christmas morning, young man, but it's only half past six. You'll wake Lucy.'

'Lucy here!' A small figure padded into her room, dragging a stocking. She smiled angelically.

'Oh — very well,' laughed Holly. 'Climb up — but shouldn't you have gone to Daddy first?'

'Thank you for the kind thought,' said an amused voice from the doorway. 'Though I suspect you have an ulterior motive!'

'Ian! What are you doing here?'

She blushed, realizing the flimsiness

of her night attire. He could laugh, standing there, an old woollen dressing-gown over his pyjamas — but she was far from adequately clad. She pulled the sheet modestly up.

'I heard Bobby, so I thought I'd join in the fun. Move up!'

He sat beside her, and as the young-sters chattered, and pushed hands into their stockings, he grinned at her discomfiture. He ruffled her dishevelled hair.

'You look delightful!' he murmured. 'Like a sleepy owl!' He ran his finger along her bare shoulder.

'Ian!' she protested in confusion. 'If I must have the whole world in my bedroom, let me make myself decent.'

With her back to him she slipped into her *négligee*, but then he whirled her around, and pulled her close against him.

'What's all the fuss about?' he chuckled. 'There's nothing I haven't seen before!'

She scrambled back into bed. 'The

stockings are being unpacked,' she chided. 'Pay a little attention, please.'

He laughed, but obeyed. Holly watched with an aching heart, as he joined in the children's play. How different he was this morning — and all because of a kiss! She shouldn't have let it happen, but she could not have helped herself. Only the timely arrival of Maggie with the cocoa had stopped things going further! At the time she hadn't cared. It had been enough that she was in his arms. Never before had she felt like this. It was madness, and she was beginning to understand the enormity of what she had done.

What would Ian say when he found she was a sham, an impostor, a . . . what was it Bobby had called her . . . a substitute! Would he hate her? Who had those kisses really been for . . . herself . . . or Carol?

'Happy Christmas, Ian,' she whispered.

He leaned forward and kissed her. A fleeting butterfly of a kiss this time, but enough to melt her resolve. Today he was happy, and so were the children, and that was the way it should be. It would be bad enough when he realized that Carol had *not* come back to him — had not even remembered her children on Christmas Day. Holly knew she could not, would not, spoil things for him today.

She smiled at him. 'Come along. Take these imps away, and let me get up. There's a lot to do today.' She shooed them out, and sprang out of bed. This was her own special day. Everything would be perfect — she was determined that it should!

After dressing she went to the east wing. Flora's rooms were just as she had imagined, in restrained good taste, and beautifully cared for.

'Anyone at home?' she asked.

'I'm in bed,' called Flora. 'I was about to get up.'

'Don't you dare!' Holly moved to the bedroom. 'How do you feel today?'

Flora grimaced. 'Pretty sore, but I'll

be all right once I'm on my feet.'

Holly examined Flora's arm. 'It will be stiff for a few days yet. Just you stay there until I bring your breakfast.'

In spite of Flora's protestations, Holly left for the kitchen where Maggie was already pushing a turkey into the oven.

★   ★   ★

That was the start of a very busy morning. So busy that she barely had time to think. It might seem strange to other people, but she had never stayed more than an odd night in an ordinary house before. Her whole life had been spent in institutions or bedsits. This was her first Christmas in a proper home, and she was enjoying every moment of it.

The kitchen, she soon discovered, was the hub of the household. As she helped prepare breakfasts, wash dishes, and peel vegetables, there was a steady coming and going of people. The children came to watch the turkey being basted, and Ian's father dropped in for a chat, only to be scolded by Maggie for lighting up his pipe.

The room was warm and bright. Its floor of red quarry tiles was covered by rush matting, and the windows looked out onto a kitchen garden, where birds squabbled in the snow over scraps of bacon rind.

Maggie moved calmly, her ample form wrapped in an apron crossed at the front and tied behind. She insisted on Holly wearing a similar garment, and made her roll up her sleeves. Together they worked, talking in low relaxed voices about the deer on the hill, the cat Snowball, blissfully baking herself against the side of the Aga, and about Bobby starting school in the village.

Studying Maggie's broad, wholesome face, Holly thought that of all the people she had ever met, she would prize this woman's opinion the most.

'Maggie,' she said tentatively. 'Have

you ever heard of people having doubles?'

Maggie lifted a heavy cloth-covered basin, containing the pudding. 'If you mean, you're not Carol MacEwan,' she said bluntly as she placed it in a saucepan, 'Aye — I've heard that!' She gave Holly a shrewd glance. 'If you mean, do I believe it — then that's another thing. I'll tell you one difference between you and Carol that's as plain as a pikestaff to me, even if others are blind to it!'

Holly stopped peeling a potato.

'It's the way you look at the master,' said Maggie. 'You're in love — and Carol wasn't. And that's the long and the short of it. Now, are we to stay bletherin' all day, or will you come and help make a bed for Mr. Malcolm?'

Holly followed her in silence. How could Maggie see so easily what she had only just realized for herself! No wonder Ian looked so jubilant. No doubt he could see what Maggie saw, but with him it only made him the more sure that she was his wife. Because he desperately wants me to be! she thought miserably. Because he is still in love with her!

* * *

The dinner was doing well, mouth-watering smells emerging from the oven. The table in the dining-room was laid, and Ian came to sharpen the carving knives, and left again after pouring them each a glass of sherry. Maggie switched on a radio, and a medley of carols added to the festivity. When the doorbell rang, Maggie had her hands in a pastry bowl, making mince pies.

'Would you answer it? It'll be Mr. Malcolm.'

Holly went with mixed feelings. She wished she knew better what the relationship between Carol and Malcolm had been. She opened the door to a flurry of snow. A burly figure was hopping about, trying to extricate its feet from what appeared to be tennis racquets.

Holly laughed. 'Hurry up in. I didn't notice it was still snowing. Maggie and I have been so busy.'

The figure proved to be a pleasant, stocky, middle-aged man with thinning hair and mild eyes. 'They're snow-shoes,' he explained. 'I thought I'd try them out, so I took a short cut across the field. They work very well, once you get the hang of it.' He looked at her, a trifle warily. 'How is Flora? Ian rang to tell me of her fall.'

Holly decided to put things straight between them. 'Flora's coming along very well,' she said. 'But before you go to her, there's something I'd like to get quite clear. Strange though it may seem, I am *not* Carol MacEwan. Even if I do look like her, it doesn't mean that I behave like her. So . . . whatever the trouble was, you have nothing to fear from me!'

He raised his eyebrows, and stood for a moment, his eyes searching her face.

'It's very hard to persuade oneself you're not Carol,' he said frankly. 'But if you say you're not, I'm prepared to take you at your word until proved wrong. Now . . . please may I go and see Flora?'

She laughed. She knew she sounded rather bossy, but she had wanted no misunderstandings. She was in quite enough difficulty as it was! She returned to Maggie and the mince pies.

'He seems a nice man,' she said, 'but although he looks so mild, I'd think he's very determined.'

'Aye! So is Miss Flora. That's the trouble!' said Maggie.

★　★　★

Christmas dinner was ready. The children joined them, and Maggie too took her place at the table, dishing up the vegetables while Ian carved the turkey, and his father poured the wine. Malcolm appointed himself Flora's left-hand man, as he called it. Ian's father said a few words of grace and then lifted his glass.

'A Happy Christmas! Here's to the family.'

'The family!'

Holly looked around the table. A family — complete — and for once she was part of it. How she wished with all her heart that it could always be so.

'This is a fine bird, Maggie,' said the old man.

'There's no charms in the pudding this year,' commented Flora. 'I thought with the children eating with us, it would be better not to have them.'

'They never did me any harm as a bairn,' complained her father. 'But then, we had the old silver threepenny pieces then. It's not the same, now they're gone.'

'I mind nearly choking on one when I was a wee child,' smiled Malcolm. 'It must have been one of the last, but it put me against pudding for years. I've got over that now, mind you,' he added hastily.

'Did you find the snow very bad, Malcolm?' asked Ian. 'What's it like on the way into town?'

'There's no getting through just now. They say the road will be cleared in a day or so. There's no trains running either. It could go on for months like this.'

Months! thought Holly. How wonderful, if only everything stayed as it was today. But the relationship between herself and Ian made that impossible. As if to underline this, she looked up to find his eyes on her, and the expression she saw there brought a flush to her cheeks. She busied herself helping Lucy, but her own eyes were drawn back to his, time and again.

When the dinner had been eaten and the pudding fetched in flaming triumph, everyone proclaimed themselves more than satisfied.

'I declare you give us more each year Maggie,' said Malcolm, patting stomach.

'If you can't over indulge this d

when can you?' laughed Flora. 'Maggie — is there anything I can do? I feel so foolish and helpless!'

'We can manage fine,' answered Maggie. 'You go to the sitting-room with the others. I know your father is dying to light up that pipe of his.'

'And I'll join him,' said Ian. 'Coming, Malcolm? When everyone's ready we'll open the presents. That's what the children are waiting for!'

Maggie began washing dishes. Holly picked up a tea towel and began to dry. It would be nice if Flora and Malcolm did marry some day, she thought. Perhaps now that Lucy was more settled Flora might feel that she could leave, if they found a nice motherly woman to look after the children. Even as the thought came into her head Holly's heart tightened painfully at the idea of leaving. They're not *my* children! she reminded herself fiercely.

She scraped some turkey scraps onto a dish for Snowball, who looked interested, stretched, sauntered to the plate, and then crouched beside it, taking quick delicate bites.

★   ★   ★

Later, Holly brought down the toys. It had been a happy thought that had made her buy them, and she could always replace them with others for the orphanage. Bobby was already investigating the parcels under the tree.

'I 'spect I know what this big one is,' he told her. 'I thought Father Christmas might bring it, but I think he's left it to Dad.'

He scampered off to fetch the others, and when they were gathered in the hall, the children were allowed to open their presents. The large parcel proved to be a big wooden sledge.

'I knew it!' squealed Bobby. 'I knew you were making it, Dad — 'cos you wouldn't let me into the shed!'

'You see too much,' chuckled Ian.

Lucy's present was a doll's cot, also made by her father, with workmanship that revealed a great love of beauty and form. The rest of the parcels were unwrapped, and from the amount of sweaters and cardigans that emerged, she could see why Flora always carried her knitting with her!

Holly was surprised when Flora picked up a small packet and held it out to her. 'It's only a wee gift . . . but then I wasn't expecting . . . '

Holly unwrapped a packet of luxury soap, which Flora had no doubt been saving for her own use. She thanked her warmly, and Flora turned an embarrassed pink.

Ian's father thrust a small box into her hand. 'From me, lassie.'

'I feel terrible,' she protested. 'I have nothing to give . . . '

She opened the box. On a velvet pad lay an intricately worked silver chain, which held a black stone. Flora caught her breath!

'Mother's iron-stone pendant!'

'Aye,' said her father. 'It was a gift from one of the family who emigrated. I believe it came from the mines in Australia. I'd like Holly to have it.'

'I couldn't accept this!' said Holly. 'It was your wife's. It should go to Flora.'

'No,' interrupted Flora. 'Father's right. I'd never wear it. You take it.'

Holly was touched by their generosity. It had been a long time since there had been anyone to give her presents, other than the odd bunch of flowers from Felix.

As they began gathering up the wrappings, Ian drew her to one side. 'Now you can have mine,' he said. 'I only finished it this morning.'

The parcel was heavy, and as Holly peeled away the layers of paper a carving was revealed, two heads carved from a single block of wood — models of the children, Lucy's elfin delicacy, and Bobby's sturdy independence faithfully portrayed. Holly stroked the faces with her finger.

'Ian . . . it's just beautiful! I shall treasure this always.'

'I'm afraid I've only the one present

for you,' he said. 'It will have to be your birthday present as well.'

'My birthday present!' She stared at him.

'You didn't think I'd forgotten? You don't deny it's your birthday today?'

'No . . . no . . . ' she faltered.

'Good. I'm glad that nonsense is over.' He put an arm around her shoulders. 'Let's join the others.'

'I'll be along in a minute, Ian. I'll just take these upstairs.'

She escaped. In her room she stared at the carving. Her birthday! She had not told Ian it was her birthday today. Nobody here knew that!

She paced the room, her mind working feverishly. There were so many questions — and the answer was so fantastic that she hardly dared voice it, even to herself! If she told Ian what she suspected, he would only accuse her of inventing even more elaborate lies. There was only one place where she could discover the truth. She *must* return to London — just as soon as the snow would allow.

The others would be wondering what had become of her. Striving to regain her composure, she went downstairs, as though nothing had happened.

The rest of the day passed pleasantly. It was still snowing lightly, and impossible to try out the new sledge. Bobby didn't mind. He was happily occupied with the caber-tossing toy.

They sat and chatted. The logs in the fireplace crackled and glowed. Nobody noticed Holly's pre-occupation. She wondered whether she should confide in Maggie, but decided against it. She could do nothing as yet. Even if the weather cleared she could not leave until Flora's arm was better.

Under the influence of the relaxed atmosphere, and liberal helpings of sherry which Ian's father kept handing round, the tension drained away from her. The old man spoke of her offer to help with his memoirs, and Ian agreed to look out a typewriter for her use. The talk turned to the old days, when the herd was started. Malcolm joined in, his arm stretched along the back of the sofa around Flora's shoulders, and Flora herself positively bloomed under his attention.

Holly knelt on the rug with Lucy, playing with her toys. Once Ian stretched out a hand and touched her hair. She looked up, startled, and he smiled lazily. She felt warm and content. It had been a wonderful day. If she could, she would have made this day last for ever.

Eventually the children were given their tea, complete with trifle, paper hats, and Christmas crackers. The adults saved their appetites for later, when it was traditional to dress for supper. Holly thought contentedly that she could wear one of those fabulous gowns! Her initial resistance to wearing Carol's clothes had worn away, and she found herself slipping little by little into the role thrust on her. This house had become her home, as no place had ever been before.

When it was time for the children to go to bed Lucy soon fell asleep, her doll tucked in bed beside her, and the lamb clutched in her arms. Bobby watched Holly as she tidied his bedroom.

'It's been a jolly good Christmas,' he remarked.

'Yes,' agreed Holly. 'It has.'

As she stood by his bedside, he put up his arms and fastened them around her neck. He pulled her head down close to his, his breath warm against her ear. 'I wish you *were* my Mummy,' he whispered.

She felt her eyelids prickle. Her arms closed tightly about his sturdy little body. 'I wish I was too, Bobby,' she said. 'But don't forget — Father Christmas only sent me for a little while.'

After she had left him, she hesitated outside Ian's door. He was still downstairs, so now was a good time to choose what she should wear for the evening. Once in his room she slid back the doors of the wardrobe. One by one she took out the evening dresses and held them against her. They were so beautiful that it was hard to choose, but she decided on a full-skirted dress of black lace, with an off-the-shoulder neckline. It would be the very thing to set off the iron-stone pendant. On a rack below she found matching shoes, and so, carrying her choices, she returned to her own room, and laid them out in readiness.

She then went to help Maggie with supper. This time they laid the table without its cloth, the polished surface reflecting the silver and glassware. They carved mounds of cold meat, prepared salads, and put out a variety of relishes and pickles. There were homemade scones, strawberry jam, rich farmhouse butter, and bowls of fruit and nuts. The pride of place was taken by a large Christmas cake.

At last Holly was able to devote time to her own preparations. She ran a bath, and lay humming a tune as she lathered herself with Flora's soap. She was looking forward to the evening. It would be nice to dress up. The nuns had not encouraged vanity in any form, but now, for the first time in her life, she found herself wishing she was beautiful.

A little later, and it seemed her wish was granted. The black dress was fantastic! Holly looked at herself in the mirror, her eyes sparkling. The neckline was more daring than she was used to, its deep frill plunging to a vee that revealed the swelling rise of her breasts, where the pendant nestled. The bodice moulded itself to her slim waist, before billowing out into a full skirt which floated with every movement. Her bare shoulders rose creamy from the black material, her slender neck supporting proudly her head with its red-gold halo.

She gave a breathless laugh, anticipating the look in Ian's eyes when he saw her. Lightly she ran down the stairs, her skirts eddying about her. She paused at the sitting-room door. Ian was alone. He was standing beside the fireplace, one arm resting on the broad stone mantelpiece, staring into the flames. Deep in thought, he did not hear her enter.

'A penny for them,' she said, a smile on her lips.

He turned, startled, and she stood with shining eyes awaiting his reaction. Then her smile faded. It was as though a shutter came down over his face. His eyes turned as cold as pebbles, and his mouth set in a hard — even cruel — line. He looked her up and down contemptuously.

'Thank you very much for reminding me,' he said coldly. 'I was fool enough to think things were different. I should have known better.'

'What's the matter . . . ' she stammered. 'Ian . . . what have I done?'

His laugh was cutting. 'Why, nothing very unexpected. We know you can behave like a slut, so it's not surprising that you dress like one.'

His gaze rested deliberately on the low neckline of her dress. 'As sluts go, you are very beautiful. Don't you think it's time your husband was allowed to sample your wares?'

He crushed her to him. With one hand he forced back her head, and then his mouth descended on hers violently, prising her lips apart. This was not how he had kissed her before. This was violation — made worse by the leaping response of her own body!

She struggled against him, but his strength was too much for her. Suddenly he was kissing her face, her neck, her breasts — roughly, cruelly. With a sharp intake of breath Holly freed one hand, and without any conscious volition on her part she gave him a resounding slap across his face. His head jerked back as he released her, his eyes widening with disbelief. She ran from the room, almost cannoning into Malcolm.

'Whoa there!' he said, steadying her. 'What's the matter?'

She pushed past him without speaking. Seeking sanctuary, she stumbled into the darkness of the library, and closed the door behind her. She fumbled her way to one of the big leather chairs. Her cheeks were scorching, her lips bruised, and scalding tears prickled beneath her eyelids.

'I will *not* cry!' she told herself, pressing her knuckles against her mouth to stop the quivering of her lips, but the tears welled up, and spilled over, trickling down her face.

The lights came on. Holly gave a cry, and covered her face with her hands. It was Malcolm who knelt beside her chair, and took her hands in his.

'It can't be all that bad!' he comforted. 'What's happened?'

Her voice catching, she repeated to him what Ian had said. 'Why has he changed so?' she asked piteously. 'It's been such a lovely day. We were all so happy — and now it's spoiled.'

Malcolm looked at her, his pleasant unassuming face troubled. 'Do you *really* have no idea?' he asked.

'Of course not,' she said with a flash

of her old spirit. 'I wouldn't be in this state if I did!'

'It's the dress,' said Malcolm. 'I'm afraid you made a bad choice there.'

She looked bewildered. 'But . . . it's a lovely dress. I know it's a little revealing, but surely not enough to make him say . . . to say . . . '

Malcolm ran his fingers through his hair. 'Last year,' he said deliberately, 'Carol wore that dress at the party. She was in a particularly bad mood. I don't know why, but whatever her motive, she . . . well, to put it bluntly, she set her cap at me.'

His face went pink. 'I was upstairs, and she came out of her room, saying her lamp was on fire. Of course, there was nothing wrong with it. She . . . she asked me to make love to her. I was horrified! Good heavens, she was Ian's wife!'

He continued, choosing his words carefully. 'I made it quite clear I wasn't interested. That made things worse. She unzipped that dress, and flung herself at me. At the same time she screamed blue murder. When the others burst in they found us struggling on the bed — and her half naked. You can imagine the scene that followed!'

'I . . . I see,' said Holly. No wonder Ian had been so angry to see her in that dress.

Malcolm pulled out a handkerchief. 'Here. Dry your eyes.'

She did as she was told, and blew her nose vigorously. She gave him a wintry grin. 'Thank you for telling me, Malcolm. I realize it wasn't easy for you.'

He patted her shoulder. 'You've got yourself into a very difficult situation here.'

'Don't I know it!' Suddenly she smiled. 'Don't worry, Malcolm. I'll survive. I think Flora is a very lucky woman — and you ought to marry her as soon as possible!'

She got up, and kissed him on the cheek.

'So! I might have guessed!'

They whirled around, transfixed at the sight of Flora, her eyes blazing. The white scarf which supported her arm was scarcely paler than her face. Her eyes were on Holly.

'I could hardly believe what Ian told me. I had to see for myself. Well . . . I know now, don't I!'

She gave a mirthless laugh. 'God help me, I was almost getting to like you! I even wondered whether I should perhaps believe you! What a fool I was. You're no different. You never will be. You are evil — that's what you are — evil!'

She swayed, and Holly gave a cry. 'Flora!' She reached out a hand.

'Get away!' Flora hissed. 'Get away from me.'

'Run along,' said Malcolm. 'You'll do no good here now. Leave it with me.'

Holly left the library, pushing past Flora, who drew away from her as though she was a leper. In her room she furiously tore off the dress and flung it into a corner. She wished she'd never set eyes on it — on any of Carol's things — even on this house!

She stood for a long time under the shower, feeling she had somehow become contaminated. She tried to be rational. She knew that Ian's anger had been directed at Carol, not herself — but she found it impossible to separate herself from it. She could not help feeling responsible. Only a few hours ago she had been one of the family. Now all that was over . . . she was alone again. She flung herself on her bed, allowing all her frustrations and longing to burst forth in a wild frenzy of sobs.

'Whisht now, Miss Holly. Don't take on so!'

Maggie's soothing tones broke into her weeping.

'Oh . . . I'm sorry, Maggie. I didn't hear you come in.' She groped for a tissue and rubbed her tear-blotched face. 'I'm sorry. This isn't like me, to cry. I don't know what came over me.'

'That's better,' said Maggie. 'Now,

come to supper.'

'Oh no!' Holly protested. 'I couldn't!'

Maggie tutted. 'So what are you going to do? Hide in your room from now on? It's all over now. Mr. Malcolm has convinced Flora that she was jumping to conclusions. And the master realizes he was hasty. He thinks you thoughtless to wear that dress — but that's all.'

'But I didn't know!' said Holly wildly. 'I had no idea . . . surely that is proof in itself. If I *was* Carol, would I be so stupid as to wear it?'

'Well . . . ' said Maggie, 'old Mr. MacEwan has said the very same thing, and Mr. Malcolm agrees. You've supporters there, my dear.'

'But I don't *want* that,' wailed Holly. 'Can't you see! I'm causing a split in the family. Maggie . . . what can I do?'

'You can come to supper,' said Maggie. 'Where's your spirit? If a thing's worth having, it's worth fighting for — remember that!'

Holly smiled wistfully. It was like an

echo from the past. She could hear Sister Agatha. 'Holly, you were a fighter when you were born, a tiny scrap not expected to live. You've been a fighter ever since . . . '

'Oh, very well,' she said. 'But I'll wear my own suit.'

Maggie was satisfied, and left. A little while later Holly went slowly back down the stairs. She returned to the sitting-room, her chin at a determined angle. Ian's father rose and put out a welcoming hand, but Ian was speaking on the telephone.

'Yes, Helen,' he was saying. 'I'd have been with you sooner, but for the snow. I promise I'll come as soon as I can. You can be sure of that.'

So he ran straight to Helen for comfort! thought Holly bleakly. Between Carol and Helen what chance have I? How can I fight . . . I don't even exist!

6

After that first awkward evening, life returned to normal, although Holly realized that nothing now would change Ian's attitude until she confronted him with proof. Flora, though wary, remained civil. Her arm improved, and soon Holly was free to devote more time to the children. At least in their company she felt at ease!

She began typing out old Mr. MacEwan's manuscript, in a corner he cleared for her in his den. She was slow at first, but soon became more adept. After a day or so, Ian developed the habit of joining them, to chat to his father. Holly enjoyed those afternoons, listening to the men's conversation. She found herself looking forward to Ian's arrival. He didn't mention that disastrous evening again, and she began to feel it had never happened.

Lucy continued to gain weight, becoming livelier every day. Sometimes Holly wrapped her up, and she and Bobby took her out into the snow, pulling her along on the sledge. They only ventured a little way, but it was enough to bring the roses back into the child's cheeks.

Occasionally Holly and Bobby went out together. Holly never tired of being out in the sweet clean air, and her eyes ever watched the hills for another glimpse of the deer, imagining how the countryside would appear when both she and the snow were gone, and the lighter green of the birch trees joined the dark firs of the plantation.

It was on one of these excursions that she was introduced to the herd — or at least a part of it. Bobby took her to a field where some of the cattle were kept. He climbed over the gate.

'They won't hurt you,' he reassured her. ''Cos they're really awfully nice.'

Holly had a city girl's healthy respect

for large animals, but she wanted to see these beasts which meant so much to Ian.

'I hope you're right, young man,' she said, as she followed him warily.

The cattle paid little attention to her, continuing to scrape at the snow with their hooves, nuzzling at the young grass beneath. Their coats were thick and matted, and long fringes of gingery hair hung down between their fearsome horns. Holly gained courage, and patted their shaggy sides, marvelling at the thickness of their coats. She could see now why Ian wanted to devote his life to them.

As though drawn by her thoughts, he came along the lane. He leaned on the gate. The herd looked up, and moved towards him.

'They know you by sight!' Holly exclaimed. 'I bet you know each one by name.'

'Naturally!' His eyes creased with laughter. 'I'm pleased to see you taking an interest in them.'

'She was frightened,' said Bobby. 'I wasn't!'

Holly laughed. 'He's right there. But I can see now that there was no need. They are beautiful!'

'They have their moments,' he said with quiet pride. 'Perhaps at long last you'll come and watch the calves when they are born.'

'I'd like that,' answered Holly, and then added wistfully, 'but I won't be here by then.'

His gaze held hers for a while. He turned to his son. 'There's a thaw forecast. If you want to try out your sledge we'd better do it this afternoon.'

'Oh boy!' Bobby bounced up and down. 'Now we'll see it go! Holly, you'll come, won't you?'

Ian lifted his son back over the gate. '*I'd* like you to come,' he said casually to Holly.

'But what about your father's book?' she protested, aware of the weakness she felt as he looked at her.

'He can spare you for an afternoon. If

144

we leave it too long the snow might be over.' His lips curled in a smile. 'Are you coming back now — or do you want to stay with the herd?'

She climbed the gate, and he lifted her down, as easily as he had his son, but he held on to one hand, his fingers curled about hers, strong and warm. Holly did not speak. She could not. The glow from her hand seemed to spread throughout her whole body.

Anyone would think we were a real family! she thought — and she ached with a longing that was hard to define.

★ ★ ★

After lunch they set off for the sledging ground. They followed the path they had taken before, but this time Bobby travelled in style. As the hill steepened Holly and Ian pulled the sledge together, floundering sometimes as they walked in the deeper snow. They paused at the point where the plantation began, to get their breath.

'It's so lovely here,' Holly panted. 'Like being on top of the world. I wish I could paint. I'd love to catch that view of the house.'

'Yes — I never tire of it. It's always changing, and yet always the same.'

He rested his arm casually across her shoulders. The gesture seemed so natural that she hardly realized it, until they moved on again through the young fir trees. Ian pointed out tracks — deer, and almost certainly fox. Above their heads a hawk hung motionless.

At last they came to the top of the ridge. Here the view was quite different, with never a tree or a sign of human habitation. The hills and gullies were softened by snow, but in the summer it would be wild and lonely country. Holly could imagine it with heather clothing its slopes.

'Here we are,' said Ian. 'You and Bobby go first.'

'Me! You're not getting me on that contraption!'

But a few minutes later, and they

were off. The sledge runners hissed and crackled on the icy surface, and it seemed they were travelling at break-neck speed, the slopes flashing by. Bobby squealed with delight. Suddenly they were at the bottom, and Holly's stomach lurched as they swooped and then rose again on the other side, until they finally came to a halt, and had to dig their feet into the snow to stop sliding backwards.

And so it continued. First one, and then the other, speeding down the hills, and climbing up again, the clear air ringing to their laughter. At last Holly's aching leg muscles forced her to a halt.

'It's all very well for you men!' she moaned, 'but if you don't wish to pull me all the way back on the sledge, I shall have to stop!'

'But, Dad,' objected Bobby, 'you haven't been down with Holly yet.'

'The sledge won't hold two adults,' said Holly.

'Oh — I think it would,' said Ian. 'If we come to pieces at the bottom, my son, you'll have to drag us *both* back!'

With the extra weight they travelled faster than ever. Ian held her tightly, his cheek against hers. There was the usual swoop at the bottom, but as they rose again the sledge tilted, spilling them onto the ground.

Breathless and laughing, Holly lay in the snow. Ian rolled on top of her, pinning her down. He raised his head, snow on his hair.

'I don't care what you say,' he gasped, his eyes burning into hers. 'You want me. I know it, and so do you!'

Holly lay still, her eyes beseeching.

'Why?' he demanded. 'I don't understand you. One minute we're so close — more than we ever were before. I can read it in your eyes — feel it in your touch. And yet you're for ever running away. Tell me you don't love me, and I'll let you go. Tell me!'

Holly struggled, but the weight of his body held her. 'Ian! Please let me up!'

'No! Not until you give me an answer.'

Holly was consumed by a crazy desire to cast all caution to the winds — to tell him she loved him — to reach up and pull him close. Indeed, her arms began to move around his neck, when she was saved by Bobby's headlong gallop down the hill. Ian cursed, and helped her up, dusting the snow from her clothes.

'It's all right,' he reassured an apprehensive Bobby. 'You won't have to pull us back after all!'

Holly was thankful for Bobby's presence. She felt shaken, as much by her own emotions as by anything else. She stole a glance at Ian as he strode beside them, his tall frame easily taking the strain of the sledge. She knew better now than to be deceived by his apparently relaxed air. He was so unpredictable! Under that calm exterior there was a volcano of passion, ready to erupt at any moment — and when it did, it fanned the flame of her own desires. Only the thought of his anger when he realized she was no more to him than a stranger, helped her to keep her head. Once he knew, he would think her contemptible for her weakness. Perhaps even accuse her of taking advantage of the situation! She felt weary and depressed. She could see no way out that would not hurt him. As for herself, life could never be the same for her again. She loved him . . . it was hopeless, but it was something she could never change.

When they reached the house he returned to the attack. Bobby ran off to tell his grandfather about the sledging, and Holly began pulling off her boots with feverish haste, but she did not escape.

'I'm waiting,' he told her. His tone was deceptively casual. 'I still haven't had my answer.'

'There isn't an answer,' said Holly, trying to keep her voice steady. 'The situation doesn't exist. You are reading things into my behaviour that aren't there.'

'Am I?' His look was sardonic. 'I

didn't mistake your reaction on Christmas Eve.'

She flushed. 'Everyone kisses everyone else on those occasions,' she retorted.

'Not like that, they don't!' His eyes mocked her, demanding the truth. 'Very well . . . leave that for the moment . . . but you *have* been happy here, haven't you?'

'Yes, Ian . . . I have.' What else could she say? It was the truth. She had never been so happy, or so miserable, as she had since she came to this house.

'Then why don't you stay? The children are happy. Father is happy. Flora could marry Malcolm. Even if you don't love *me*, isn't it worth staying for everyone's sake? If we worked at it, couldn't we build a marriage that was worthwhile?'

Her heart felt as though it would break. Why not? she thought wildly. Carol would never come back — so who would know. She loved them all so much — could it be wrong to make so many people happy?

The arguments were strong. Everyone insisted she was Ian's wife. She only had to admit it, and her life could be spent with him. She would be a good mother to the children — a good wife to Ian. She could give him a love he had never found with Carol. He need never know his happiness was founded on a lie. What choice had she now . . . without him she had nothing!

The idea was subtly compelling. Holly closed her eyes, her face drained of colour.

'I'm sorry, Ian . . . it's impossible.'

'Impossible — why?' There was a ragged edge to his voice now. Any minute, and he would explode again.

'Ian, there's no point in continuing this conversation. When the thaw comes I must go to London. Then everything will become clear.'

His face darkened. She could see a pulse beating in his neck. 'You want to see this Felix fellow, I suppose! What is the hold he has over you?'

'Felix!' She almost laughed. 'This has nothing to do with him. Ian, please! Don't let's talk about it again until I've been to London.'

He turned as if to walk away, and then swung around, pointing an accusing finger. 'Your place is with us. You're staying here where you belong. You're not running off again to London or anywhere else . . . I'll see to that!'

He stalked off up the stairs, and she heard the door of his bedroom slam.

Holly gave a sigh of relief. She hurried to telephone Felix. There was always the chance that he might be at home now, since he worked strange hours at the hospital. As it happened, she was in luck.

'Oh Felix — I'm sorry if I've disturbed you. I hope you weren't asleep.'

'Holly — sweetheart! Where on earth *are* you? I've had a terrible time here. Absolutely nobody intelligent to talk to. It's too bad of you, deserting me.'

It was good to hear his light, flippant voice again.

'I'm sorry, Felix dear — but you'll have to manage a little longer. I won't be back yet. I'm snowed in.'

'Ha! What did I tell you!' he crowed. 'You wouldn't listen! Well — I hope you're enjoying your diet of porridge, and are wearing your long woolly drawers!'

'Felix!' she laughed. 'Be serious for a moment. Listen ... there's a thaw coming, and the trains may be running again soon. When I come, could you give me a bed for the night? Mrs. Barnes is using my room.'

'My dear, I'd be delighted. Haven't I been trying to get you into bed for months!'

'You're incorrigible! I mean a bed in your spare room. Only for a night, Felix. I can't explain now, but I'll see you as soon as I can. Leave the spare key on its usual ledge.'

The phone was snatched from her hand. Ian had heard her last few words.

'Listen to me, Felix whoever you are!' he snarled into the receiver. 'My wife stays here! Keep away from her in future, or you'll have me to answer to!' He slammed down the phone and glared at Holly. 'Now he knows just where he stands!'

'He surely does — you made sure of that!' Holly had a vision of Felix's dumbfounded amazement. She felt a hysterical giggle rising. It was too much — she could not hold it back. She began to shake helplessly, while tears of mirth ran down her cheeks.

Ian stared in anger. 'There's nothing funny about it!' he growled.

'No . . . there isn't!' she gasped, but she could not stop. 'I'm sorry . . . I'm going upstairs!'

She fled, leaving him staring after her.

⋆   ⋆   ⋆

The week passed, and New Year's Eve was upon them. Here Hogmanay was

155

even more important than Christmas. A few guests had, after all, been invited — a couple of farming friends of the old man's, and the minister and his wife, and of course, Malcolm. The weather was warmer, and though the lane was still full of snow, it was no longer crisp. The visitors left their cars on the top road, and struggled down to the house on foot, arriving wet and exhausted.

They brought with them the news that trains would be running the following morning, and it was probable that the milk train would be stopping at the town station. She would have to make plans, thought Holly. She felt sure that Ian would stop her leaving if he could. She deliberately avoided being alone with him. The weather proved an ally. It was not fit to go outside, and she always contrived to be with other people. As ever, though, Ian's anger was short-lived.

He insisted, however, that she should join their guests for dinner, and she agreed on condition that *he* chose what she should wear. She was determined not to make yet another blunder. She was well pleased with his choice, a white dress which clung to the supple lines of her young body, leaving one shoulder bare. It was simple, but effective, and Holly felt confident that she looked her best when she joined the others.

Old Mr. MacEwan's friends were farmers, wind-reddened and stocky. Holly dubbed them 'Tweedle Dum and Tweedle Dee'. The minister was a tall, vague, dark man, well under the thumb of his affectionately cheerful wife.

The talk centred on farming matters and church functions, jumble sales, and fat stock prices, children and recipes. Holly was surprised to find herself taking part. How different from conversations with Felix's friends, who could argue for hours on the nuances of the latest play. Here it was the fundamentals of life that mattered, and she found them just as interesting!

In the evening the men got together, talking men's talk, while the women concerned themselves with the really important topics of who had died, had a baby, or been married recently. The logs burned brightly, having a soporific effect. It was all Holly could do to keep her eyes open. A few minutes before midnight Ian's father filled all their glasses.

'What's this?' asked Holly, eyeing the golden liquid.

'Liquid gold!' chuckled the old man. 'You must have a wee dram to see in the New Year.'

They stood, their glasses at the ready, watching the grandfather clock, as its minute hand moved towards the hour. It began to strike, and on the last note there was a pounding at the front door, and there was the minister with a lump of coal in one hand, and a bottle of whisky in the other. He must have stolen out to perform the first footing, though Holly had not noticed him go.

Then there were cries of 'Happy New

Year'. Everybody was kissing everyone else. Even Flora gave Holly a peck on the cheek, and there was the linking of hands and the singing of 'Auld Lang Syne'. Before they returned to the warmth of the sitting-room, they had one more wee dram from the bottle.

Holly began to feel quite dizzy. She sat on a corner of the sheepskin rug, her feet tucked under her, gazing into the fire. She was hardly aware of the visitors making their goodbyes and drifting away. As if in a dream she found herself shaking hands, and then resumed her sleepy seat before the flames.

'Well — I'm off to my bed,' said Ian's father. 'Will you be sure to lock up, Ian?'

'Goodnight,' said Holly. 'And a Happy New Year.'

The old man hugged her. 'You're a good wee lassie,' he said.

As he left, Holly stifled a yawn. 'I must be off too.'

'No — wait a minute,' said Ian. 'I

want to play a record I think you'll like.' As the soft strains of the music began, he joined her on the rug.

'I'm curious to know what you see in those flames,' he said. 'When I was small I'd sit for hours looking into them.'

Holly smiled. There had been no real fires when she was a child — only a monstrous old iron boiler and ugly grey radiators, but she knew what she would have seen, if she *had* looked into one. 'Just a home,' she said. 'A house — and a family.'

His fingers began stroking her bare shoulder, gentle and soothing. 'Well — you have all those things now.'

She felt the danger signals, but she felt strangely languid. 'Ian . . . ' she began slowly. 'Suppose . . . just suppose you'd never been married, and that you met me for the first time today. What do you think would happen?'

'What do you mean?'

Her forehead wrinkled, as she strove to find the words. 'What would you have felt, if you'd met me this Christmas for the very first time? Would you perhaps have passed me by, without even a second glance?'

'What a question!' He gave a puzzled laugh. 'How can one separate the present from the past? I would have fallen in love with you, just the same.'

She turned to him, her face serious. 'Would you, Ian? With *me*, the girl who is here now . . . not the girl you married? Are you sure?'

He bent his head, and his lips brushed her shoulder. 'You talk in riddles. I love you — now — and I always will. Isn't that enough?'

He pulled her to him, and gently laid her on the softness of the rug, lying with his body close to hers, the warmth of the fire on her back. She returned his kisses as though in a dream. The past, the future — they did not matter. Only this moment was real.

She answered his endearments with her own words of love she had held back for so long. His fingers fumbled for the zip of her dress, and as his hands began stroking the silky skin of her back, she was drawn into a whirlpool of sensation, with neither the desire nor the strength to withdraw. Soon, she knew, she would be lost forever — and yet she still lay as if under a spell, unable to save herself.

'I love you,' he whispered again and again, and as he began to slide the silken sheath of her dress from her other shoulder, she offered no resistance. His hand cupped her breast.

'You've been driving me crazy,' he murmured. 'I've tried to hold back, afraid of frightening you away again. Now I know you are mine. Carol . . . my darling!'

'No! No!' The wild cry burst from her lips, as she was brutally brought back to reality. Her dream was shattered, and the spell which held her was broken. She pushed him from her, and scrambled trembling to her feet.

Ian jumped up too. He was white with frustrated anger. 'What the devil's wrong now?' he demanded.

'I'm *not* Carol . . . I'm *not*!' she cried. 'Haven't I told you so a hundred times. I'm *not* your wife . . . I'm me. I'm Holly!'

'So you're still playing games!' His voice was trembling with emotion. 'Does it give you a thrill to see what power you have over me? God knows why I care for you. You are nothing but a cheap little tease. Well, it's a dangerous game to play!'

'What . . . what are you doing?'

He jerked her off her feet, so that she fell face down across his knees. 'I'm teaching you a lesson,' he sneered, as he began to spank her with the full weight of his arm. 'I'll teach . . . you to . . . play games . . . with me!'

The indignity made her numb to the stinging slaps. She kicked and wriggled, but he held her firm. He did not let her go until his arm was tired, and his anger spent. At last she was free, facing him, her face red, her breasts heaving.

'You'll be sorry, Ian MacEwan,' she

said bitterly. 'Believe me — you'll regret this.'

'You only got what you deserved,' he mocked, a devil in his eyes. 'That's what happens to young ladies who lead a man on.'

'Lead a man on . . . ' She almost choked in her fury. 'What about you . . . plying me with whisky, and trying to seduce me!'

'Seduce you! Seduce my own wife!' He laughed. 'That's not a bad idea.

He took a step towards her, a glint in his eyes, and she panicked and ran — his laughter ringing in her ears.

★   ★   ★

By the time she reached her own room her mind was made up. She could not remain in the same house as Ian for a moment longer. It was not that she feared him, but she knew that sooner or later, if she stayed, she would succumb to the promptings of her heart. She must run, while there was still time.

She removed the white dress, and pulled on slacks and a heavy sweater. She heard Ian coming along the passage, and froze until she heard his door shut. Then she hurriedly scribbled a note for Maggie. Luckily she knew that Maggie would be about long before the children stirred.

After that, it only remained for her to put a few things into her overnight bag, and she was ready. It was already one-thirty in the morning. She checked her purse. She had enough for a return ticket to London, but not much to spare. She wouldn't be able to afford a taxi to the town. Surely she could walk there in time for the milk train? She wished now that she had a clearer idea of the distance involved. She would have to chance it.

Gathering up her things, she crept into Lucy's room, and kissed the sleeping child. 'I'll be back, baby,' she whispered. 'I promise!'

She opened the door cautiously. Holding her breath, she slipped out.

She tiptoed down the corridor, and slipped the note under Maggie's door, and then felt her way down the stairs, step by step. There was enough moonlight filtering into the hall for her to be able to grope for her anorak and boots. She came across Malcolm's showshoes, and picked them up. Clutching them, she opened the front door.

She hesitated for a second, as the cold air hit her. She was leaving this house, with all it held that was dear to her. When she returned, things would be very different.

She stepped over the threshold, closing the door behind her.

7

Holly followed the moonlit path, slipping on the wet snow. The world was shadowy silence, and the air smelled of night. The lane sloped steeply to where it met the top road. There, Holly knew, she must turn right and follow the road to where it joined the main highway. There the going might be easier.

She kept her eyes on the dark ruts, until she came to a gate she knew from her walks with Bobby. She looked back at the house, a dark mass below. It felt strange, knowing that nobody was aware of her absence. Strange — and rather frightening.

She remembered that if she climbed the gate, and crossed the field, she could meet up with the road further on, and the undisturbed snow would be easier than the water-filled ruts of the lane. By the pale moonlight she could see the far corner of the field quite clearly, and once she had fixed the snowshoes to her boots, she launched herself towards it. Malcolm had been right — it was not easy!

At first she stumbled, until she developed a swinging rhythm. Head down, she moved doggedly forward, ignoring the muscles that were beginning to protest. Then clouds obscured the moon, and glancing up she saw that she could no longer see the boundary of the field. Even as she stared the darkness closed in.

She stood, reluctant to step out blindly, and yet it would be as bad to try to retrace her steps as it was to go forward. It was eerie, advancing into nothing. All sound was blanketed by the snow, except for her own laboured breathing. She pushed on with grim determination. Suppose I am walking in circles! she thought. She had heard of such things happening. But after a while, the moon came out again, and she saw the top of the field. With a heartfelt prayer of thanks, she found the gate, and climbed into the road.

Her legs were trembling. The turmoil of emotion which had carried her out of the house had drained away, and she realized the task she had set herself. It would be more sensible to go back, but she could picture Ian's reaction if she hammered on the door to be let in — it didn't bear thinking about! She steeled herself to set off again.

The trees cast pools of blackness across her path. The pinpoints of stars emphasized her insignificance, and she was filled with a sense of isolation. It was as though she were suspended between two worlds — that of Ian and the family, and the other, the world of London and Felix.

She walked on mechanically, filled with thoughts elusive and yet persistent. Icy slush soaked through her boots, and her whole body was growing numb. She pulled herself together with a jerk, to realize that she had been falling asleep.

In the east the sky was lightening. As yet she had not even reached the main road, and when she did it would still be a long way to the town. One thing was certain — she had to keep moving. What a fool she had been to undertake this headlong flight!

Then Holly stood still. She had become aware of a noise — a distant low humming sound. At first she imagined Ian was pursuing her in the Landrover — but then she saw how unlikely this was. He would surely still be in bed and sound asleep. She stepped into the deeper snow at the side of the road and waited. Now she could see the approaching lights of a heavy juggernaut. It was nearly upon her when she stepped forward into the dazzle of its lights, waving her arms. She caught a glimpse of a startled face as it ploughed past. Then she heard the brakes come on.

Holly pounded after it. As she reached it, a light came on in the cab. 'Grab hold of that there handle to your right. That's it, flower — put your left foot on the step . . . can you manage?'

'Yes . . . yes thank you.'

Holly threw her bag up, and clambered after it, slamming the door. Immediately the lights went out. She heard the hiss of the brakes being released, and they were off.

'I'm running to the station yard in Glasgow. Is that any use to you?'

'Oh yes!' said Holly. 'That would be wonderful . . . thank you so much.'

Her worries were over, for the time being. There would be no need to worry about the milk train now. She relaxed, sinking back into the springy seat. The cab smelled of diesel fuel and warm plastic, but it was cosy and secure. Before she knew it she was dozing, while the truck thundered on.

She eventually awoke to find they had stopped, and her companion was pouring steaming coffee from a thermos.

'I always break the journey at this layby,' he explained, handing her a mug. 'Have a sandwich. The wife makes far too many, just in case.'

She accepted the drink gratefully. She was stiff, and aware of hunger stirring. She took a thick wedge of bread and cheese. She could see the driver clearly now, a big man, filling the driver's seat to overflowing, dressed in dark green overalls with the firm's name on the breast pocket.

When they continued their journey he told her about his life on the road, the long hauls across the country, his nights away from home, riding lonely through the darkness.

'I ring the missus every night,' he said. 'She's a good'un my wife. I've seen too many men fretting about what might be happening back home. That's no use in this job . . . you need your wits about you. A family — I reckon that's what keeps a man steady.'

Holly agreed, and her thoughts flew to the family she had just left. They would be waking now. She hoped Maggie was with Lucy when she awoke.

And what would Ian be thinking? She remembered again, with a sudden leaping of the blood, the urgency of his body against hers, only hours ago. On her return, what would his reaction be?

At the station in Glasgow, her new friend bluntly refused to accept the money she offered. 'I was glad of the company,' he said. 'Take care now. I wouldn't go wandering off at night again, flower, if I were you. It's a risky business, taking lifts. I don't usually offer them — but I couldn't leave you in the snow.'

The station had that grey empty air that all stations have. It was cold, and as the minutes ticked by, any warmth Holly had gained in the lorry, slowly seeped away from her. It was a relief when the train slid in to the station. Then she was aboard it, settling herself into a seat by the window. Doors slammed. A whistle blew. They began to move. At last, she was really and truly on her way.

During the long journey Holly was

too busy with her thoughts to pay much attention to the scenery. Sometimes she dozed. Because of the lift she had a little money to spare, and at lunch time she made her way unsteadily to the dining-car, and sat there at a solitary meal, staring out of the window. What if this was all a wild-goose chase? And if she was no wiser at the end of it — what then? She refused to let the idea take root. For better or worse, she *must* know the truth before nightfall.

After an eternity the train drew into King's Cross, and Holly collected her belongings, and pushed her way through the crowds, becoming aware for the first time that her clothes hardly fitted the London scene. Her bulky anorak and trousers tucked into water-stained boots were causing glances of amusement. Goodness knows what Felix would say. He liked his women to be stylish and well-groomed. Still — there was nothing she could do about it now. The afternoon was already well advanced, and she had hardly begun.

The next step of her journey took her by bus towards Islington. She was afraid she would not recognize the place she was seeking, it had been so long since she had been there. But at last she saw a familiar landmark — the long high wall of St. Margaret's Convent, stretching in a great curve on one side of the tree-lined street. As she jumped down from the bus she felt sure that behind those walls lay the answers to all her questions.

Holly did not recognize the young nun who admitted her, but the smell of the bare white corridors awoke memories, and the echoing of her feet as she followed the grey-robed figure was as familiar to her as her own breath. It felt strange to be back.

She sat in the Mother Superior's empty office, her ears straining for the sounds of the children who would be at lessons behind the closed doors. Time seemed to stand still in this room. How often had she been summoned here, after one of her many indiscretions! The same text hung on the wall. The same shelves of books lined the space behind the desk. The same devotional pictures looked down on her with gentle disinterest. She fidgeted, remembering past guilt of other occasions.

The door opened, and she rose to her feet, her face lighting in a smile. 'Sister Agatha! I didn't expect to see you. Oh, it *is* good to meet you again!'

Grey eyes smiled into hers, and robes rustled as the familiar figure seated itself behind the desk.

'I'm Mother Superior now, Holly,' said the well-remembered voice. 'What can I do for you, child?'

Holly felt a surge of relief. The old Mother Superior had always seemed so awe-inspiring — but Sister Agatha was quite different! Holly came to the crux of the matter without more ado.

'There is something I *must* know. Sister . . . I mean, Mother Superior . . . before my mother died in that hospital, did she have another baby?

Was I . . . was I one of twins?'

The words hung heavy between them. The nun opened a file she had brought with her. She turned the papers over as though debating what to say. She looked up.

'Well, my dear — there seems no good reason for refusing an answer, now. Yes, there *were* two children born on that Christmas Day. Identical twins — yourself, and your sister, Carol.'

Holly let out her breath. This was the information she had been expecting, and yet its realization was a shock.

'Why wasn't I told?' she cried. 'All those years! You had no right to deny me the knowledge of my own sister!'

The nun looked at her, a certain twinkle in her eyes. 'Calm yourself, Holly — still as impetuous as ever, I see!' She leaned back in her chair, her face serene.

'You must remember that matters regarding adoption were very different in those days. As it happened, Carol was born first. She was a strong healthy baby. Unfortunately you were not. Indeed, it was not expected that you would survive. We had a young couple eagerly awaiting a baby for adoption. We could not deny Carol her chance. She was gone before you came from hospital. Later there seemed no point in telling you about a sister you would never see. It seemed best to leave things alone.'

Holly bowed her head. 'It would have saved a lot of trouble if I *had* known,' she said. 'You have no idea of the complications it has caused.'

The Mother Superior smiled calmly. 'I have always found, Holly, that when things get complicated it is because people have made them so.' She looked at Holly, her head on one side. 'Are you sure you have not done your share?'

Holly was silent. The nun went on. 'I believe the family moved. Are you quite certain that it is wise to seek your sister after all this time?'

'I *would* like to find her,' answered Holly, 'but not for myself. It's far too late for that now!' She stopped for a moment, in danger of becoming emotional. 'No . . . I just need to have written proof. That is what I have come for.'

The nun took a brown envelope from the file. 'I guessed what your visit must be for. These are photostat copies of both birth certificates, and your mother's death certificate. I imagine they will be sufficient for your requirements.' A smile touched her eyes. 'Oh yes . . . we are quite up-to-date, you know.'

Without speaking, Holly took the envelope, and tucked it into her bag. The Mother Superior rose to her feet. 'Before you go, I am sure you would like to look around.'

Holly followed her. Where were they all now? she wondered. The children she had known when she lived here? In her old dormitory she looked around her wistfully.

'You've had new curtains. It looks very pretty — but everything's changed.' She felt vaguely resentful.

'Life moves on — even here,' said Mother Superior.

She walked back along the corridors with Holly, and out as far as the wrought-iron gate. She put her hands on Holly's shoulders, and kissed her fondly on both cheeks.

'You were always a wayward child — but your heart was good. Follow your instinct. Whatever is troubling you, the way will become clear. The Lord works in mysterious ways!'

*　*　*

He certainly does! sighed Holly, as she took the bus back to Felix's flat. For the moment she felt incapable of coherent thought. By the time she stood on Felix's doorstep, she was in a state of exhaustion. She was fumbling for the key, when the door opened, and she stumbled into Felix's arms.

'Holly — my pet! Why didn't you say you were coming? Good heavens — what's been going on in those godforsaken parts? You look like a waif and stray!'

He stood, tall and immaculate, a look of astonishment on his smooth fair face. To his utter consternation Holly burst into tears against his chest. Half laughing, half crying, she allowed him to shepherd her in.

'Pay no attention to me,' she gasped. 'I'm just dead beat. I was walking most of the night!' She stood in a daze, obedient as a child, as she allowed him to unzip her anorak and remove it.

How wavy his blond hair is! she thought vaguely. Almost too perfect — but he *is* kind — I had forgotten how kind!

'The first thing you need, my girl, is a nice hot bath.' He pushed her into the bathroom. 'Use my robe — that's it hanging on the door. Are you sure you can manage — or shall I undress you?'

She made a funny little noise, that might have been a giggle or a sob. 'Bless you, Felix. I shall be all right.'

He left, and she peeled off her

clothes. In the warmth of the water she closed her eyes, and revelled in the comfort it brought. Then she amused herself by counting his expensive soaps and lotions. Felix certainly didn't stint himself. She could not imagine Ian using such things.

Ian! The memory stabbed her.

'I say — Holly!' The door opened a discreet crack. 'When did you last eat?'

'Well . . . I had a lorry driver's bread and cheese at five this morning, and a British Rail lunch.'

'Just as I thought. Barbaric! How does a Spanish omelette strike you — with a bottle of Niersteiner to wash it down? It will only take about ten minutes.'

'Heavenly,' agreed Holly. She sank further below the water, stirring the bubbles with her toes.

She allowed herself another five minutes of luxury, and then, feeling decidedly more human, she slipped into the bath robe. The sleeves were too long, and she rolled them up. She half registered the fact that the telephone was ringing, but did not pay it much attention, until Felix's responses began to get through to her.

'Yes . . . she's here. Could you hang on while I see if she's dressed . . . what do you mean! Now look here . . . I don't know what you're talking about!'

Silence. Then she heard Felix replace the receiver. She opened the door. 'Was that for me, Felix?'

He gave an embarrassed grin. '*That* — apparently — was your husband! No . . . say no more! I must save our meal from complete incineration. After that we'll talk!'

True to his word Felix did not allow her to speak until she had tucked into a delicious omelette, lifted sizzling from the pan. There was a basket of warm bread rolls, and exquisitely cut glasses of chilled white wine. Holly ate appreciatively, but her mind was buzzing with speculation.

'Felix!' she said at last. 'You must tell me what Ian had to say.'

He raised his eyebrows. 'Ian is it? He sounded like Attila the Hun! Tell me, my sweet, just when did you marry this fiery Scot?'

There was an unaccustomed edge to his usually urbane voice. Holly shook her head with exasperation. 'Don't be silly, Felix. Of course I'm not married to him — but he *thinks* I am!'

Felix's jaw dropped, and then he recovered his poise. He lifted a table napkin, and touched his lips. 'How on earth could a man think he was married to you, if he wasn't? I'm damn sure I'd know the difference!'

'It's a long story.'

'There's plenty of time,' said Felix. So — she had to begin at the beginning — at the day she left the coach, when it had all started. She told him all, except for the way she had come to feel about Ian.

'So you see,' she concluded. 'It's quite simple, really.'

'Simple!' Felix gave a snort of derision. 'My dear girl, if you call that simple you need your head examining. It's all too bizarre! I don't believe a word of it.'

She picked up her bag, and took out the envelope. 'Proof,' she said. 'There's no doubt. Carol and I are identical twins.'

She then handed him the note she had found in her anorak, the day she had climbed the hill for the Christmas tree. 'This is the note I found. There's not much to go on.'

Felix scrutinized the documents. He leaned back in his chair. He sipped his wine, his eyes considering her.

'It seems to me you're well out of it. You've been pretty foolish — but there's no need to go back. Just post these, and everyone will understand.'

'I couldn't do that!' said Holly. 'I must go back.'

Felix buttered a cream cracker, and cut a thin wedge of Danish blue. 'Why must you? I want you here. There's a new production of 'The Doll's House' just starting. And Marge and Geoffrey are throwing a party. You owe these people nothing. What happens from now on is not your concern. You'd be mad to go anywhere near this MacEwan chap — the way he sounded!'

'But what did he say!' protested Holly. 'Was he very angry?'

Felix gave a short laugh. 'He was about to jump down the phone and throttle me with his bare hands. Apparently he'd followed your tracks — something about wandering drunkenly round a field.'

Holly's cheeks burned. 'Of all the nerve!' she exploded. 'I was *not* drunk. I just couldn't see.'

Felix shrugged. 'I merely repeat his words, my dear. He'd been scouring the countryside, worried stiff. Then he found my address in the book you left behind you. He'd been ringing all day, but I was at work.'

Holly's indignation subsided. A glow spread through her. So Ian had worried about her! She reached out and touched Felix. 'You've been wonderful,' she smiled. 'But you see, I feel I owe it to him to tell him in person. After all, Carol is my sister . . . somehow that makes me feel responsible.'

Felix took on a stubborn look. 'A couple of weeks ago you didn't even know she existed! You belong here, Holly. This is your background, your kind of world. Forget this nonsense!'

Holly shook her head with a mixture of affection and exasperation. It was not true, what he had said about her belonging here in his world — she knew that now. She had never felt, with him, that completeness of belonging she had experienced in Scotland. 'No, Felix,' she said with determination. 'I have to go back.'

For a moment he looked angry, but it passed, as though he could not be bothered to hold on to such a disagreeable emotion. He shrugged. 'All right,' he conceded. 'But if you must go, wait until I can go with you. I'd feel happier about it.'

'No,' said Holly. 'The sooner I do this the better.'

Felix's sigh held a trace of exasperation. 'Very well — but I don't like it. After all ... I thought we meant something to one another.' He held up a hand to stop her speaking. 'No ... I see you have to get this out of your system. Go along to your uncouth Scot, but I don't know what sort of a welcome you think you'll get. Your 'husband's' last words were, 'Tell her I've finished with her for good. She need never set foot in this house again!' It hardly sounds as though he'll be pleased to see you back!'

A light died in Holly's eyes. 'Nevertheless,' she said steadily, 'no matter what he thinks of me ... I'm going back!'

8

The next day Holly decided to visit her landlady, and pick up a change of clothes. She told Felix of her plans, as they sat down to breakfast. If he was ruffled by the events of the previous night he certainly did not show it.

'You're looking better this morning,' he remarked. 'If I may offer a free medical opinion, I'd say you've been living on your nerves too much. Can't I persuade you to drop this mad idea?'

Holly grinned. 'You make very good coffee, Felix — but you can't change my mind.'

A look of irritation crossed his bland features. 'Come off it, my sweet,' he snapped. 'There's no real reason to go. You could easily deal with matters by post. You're being pig-headed. Or is there something you haven't told me?'

Holly flushed. 'Whatever reasons I

may have, Felix,' she replied with dignity, 'they are my own. You don't have the right to dictate to me!'

He sighed. 'Very well. I haven't time to argue. I must be off to the hospital. If you need to come back you know you'll be very welcome.'

Holly regretted her outburst. She knew he was speaking out of concern for her. Before he left she kissed him.

'I'm sorry,' she said. 'I didn't mean to bite your head off. I can't thank you enough for what you've done.'

He pulled a wry face. 'I get the distinct feeling that I've missed the boat with you, Holly my dear. It's my own fault. I took you for granted . . . and now you've changed.'

Holly did not know how to answer him. 'Felix — I'm truly sorry.'

He raised her hand to his lips. 'Don't be!' he said airily. 'I haven't given up hope yet.'

After he had gone Holly tidied the flat. It was, she thought, the least she could do to repay his hospitality. Felix had flair — she had to admit that. She stood, her head on one side, considering one of his more futuristic paintings. It fitted this environment, but would have been horribly out of place in Ian's home.

A wave of longing swept over her. Up there the children would be starting another day. Maggie would be busy in the kitchen — Flora setting the house to rights — Father lighting up his pipe. And Ian . . . he would be striding down the lane to inspect the herd, hands thrust deep into the pockets of his old tweed jacket, head thrown back, his eyes searching the hills gauging the weather for the coming day.

★　★　★

When Holly arrived at her bed-sit, she had another shock awaiting her.

'Now — isn't this nice, ducky!' Mrs. Barnes poured tea into two Coronation mugs. 'It was a surprise to see you! I was just saying to our Marlene, I reckon

Holly has gone for good, I said . . . '

'Your daughter? Has her husband had any luck with a job?'

'Well, yes!' Mrs. Barnes leaned forward confidentially. 'As a matter of fact he has. That's the trouble! Well — they need somewhere to live, don't they — and our Marlene has a little one on the way, so it makes it hard for them, you see.' Her eyes flickered away, embarrassed. 'So . . . it'd be easier for you, ducky — as you're on your own — so I told them you wouldn't mind if they stayed!'

Holly was shattered. Her room had not been much — but it was the only home she had. Mrs. Barnes bridled.

'I'm sorry, dearie . . . but you do understand. Flesh and blood have to come first!'

There was nothing Holly *could* say, except that she understood. She sipped her tea morosely. Mrs. Barnes looked relieved.

'I knew you would. I said, to Marlene, I said . . . '

Holly interrupted the flow. 'I wanted to pick up some clothes.'

'Oh well, now!' Mrs. Barnes looked disconcerted. 'You see, I've packed all your stuff into cardboard boxes. It wasn't as if you had all that much, dearie, did you? You're welcome to leave them here until you get settled.'

So! That's it then, thought Holly, as she made her way back to the station. No job, no home — and certainly no knowing what awaited her in Scotland.

All the same, on board the train her spirits began to rise. She watched the countryside flashing by, and felt a flutter of excitement. She was going home. She knew this feeling was illogical, but something in that wild countryside was drawing her back.

To pass the time she took out the birth certificates. Maureen Fraser . . . her mother. Carol Fraser . . . her sister. *They* were her real family, and yet to her they were just names on pieces of paper. She closed her eyes, in an attempt to feel some inner response

— but there was nothing. Her mother was a shadowy figure. As for Carol . . . how could she have treated Ian so badly? How could she turn her back on her own children? She had everything I ever wanted, thought Holly with unaccustomed bitterness — and she threw it all away!

She tucked the certificates back in their envelope. When Ian read these he would understand at last that Carol had truly gone. How would he take such finality? Would he realize that these past weeks had not belonged to Carol, but to her . . . to Holly? Would he then look at her with different eyes?

Her stomach fluttered again, and to escape her thoughts she engaged in conversation with a woman whose small child was busy sticking chewing-gum to the carriage window.

When she changed trains at Glasgow, Holly telephoned the Hall, and it was Maggie who answered. Her relief at hearing Holly's voice was warming to the heart.

'Oh, my dear, it will be good to have you safe home. Did you find what you were looking for?'

'I did,' said Holly. 'But I'll tell you later. I have to go now, Maggie. Could you ask Ian if he'd meet me at the station — I've no money for a taxi.'

'I'm sorry — but he's away out for the evening. Don't worry — I'll see there's somebody to meet you.'

There was a pause. 'Do you know where he's gone?' asked Holly. Over the phone she could hear Maggie's disapproving sniff.

'I believe he did say something about seeing Helen.'

★   ★   ★

Holly spent the rest of the journey warmed by her own indignation. After all her efforts on his behalf, to find that he had hardly waited a minute before running for comfort to that . . . that glamour puss! Well — let him!

When Malcolm met her at the end of

her journey, she gave him no more than a brief greeting until they were on their way back.

'I'm surprised Flora allowed *you* to come for me!'

He chuckled. 'There was no-one else available.' He glanced at her with mild curiosity. 'Are you aiming to make a habit of this kind of thing? You had them all in a terrible state!'

'I know,' said Holly with quick contrition. 'I'm afraid I didn't stop to think that anyone might worry — but it was worth it. I've got what I went to find.'

She gave a quick explanation of the events surrounding her birth. He gave a low whistle.

'So that was it! Well . . . I suppose it certainly puts the record straight. But, my dear, where do *you* go from here?'

'That's the trouble,' said Holly slowly. 'I've no idea!'

They drove in silence, and arrived at the Hall after stopping to retrieve the snowshoes. Maggie hurried Holly into the kitchen.

'The bairns are in bed,' she said. 'You can see the others in a wee while, but you need a rest and a bite to eat.'

So, sitting at the bare deal table, Holly told her tale to Maggie. When it was finished, the older woman rose to replenish the heavy brown teapot.

'I'll not say I'm surprised,' she remarked. 'There had to be an explanation for the likeness. We never realized Carol was adopted, you know. Perhaps that's why her parents spoiled her so. It's natural too, that you should turn up here — after all, we are on the tourist route. Most people visit here some time in their lives.'

She patted Holly on the shoulder. 'When you've finished that will you be telling the others? I rather think they'll be hoping to hear what you have to say.'

Holly was reluctant to leave the security of the kitchen. Until then she had been buoyed up by the success of her mission — but now she had her answers she was strangely reluctant to reveal them. Her acceptance in the family had been paid for with her sister's identity. Without that, she was shorn of any right to be here at all.

'Run along,' said Maggie. 'Best get it over.'

When she went into the sitting-room old Mr. MacEwan drew her near to the fire. 'Flora — give the child a wee dram. You must be fair exhausted with all your travelling.'

Flora poured out a generous whisky. Malcolm was lounging back in one of the armchairs, watching them. He saw Holly's uncertainty, and made it easier for her.

'I've already told them,' he said.

Holly sank into a chair. The flames leaped, throwing warm shadows on the wall, and across the faces of those looking at her. As the whisky sent warmth coursing through her veins, she knew that she was not the only one who felt on edge.

'Well . . . ' she said with a brief laugh.

'There's nothing much more I can say. Carol and I were . . . are . . . identical twins. She was taken for adoption at birth — but I was brought up at the Home.'

Flora twiddled a glass in her fingers, her head bent. 'Holly, I owe you an apology. I shan't blame you if you say 'I told you so'. You did . . . many times . . . but I was too stubborn to believe you!'

'Aye — and I told you so, too. But then no-one ever listens to me!'

'Oh, Father! There's no need to sound so hard done by!' In spite of her scolding there was affection in Flora's voice. 'What we have to worry about now is how Ian is going to react.'

Holly looked at her questioningly. Flora continued: 'Your coming brought Ian to life again. He was a different man. I was beginning to hope . . . well, never mind that now. When you went off again, I thought he'd lose his reason. I tell you, I don't know how he'll take this!'

Malcolm squeezed her hand. 'Don't worry so, Flora. Ian isn't a child.'

Holly made her excuses, and left them — wanting to escape their kindliness. I don't deserve it! she thought. I've given Ian hope — only to destroy it. I'm just as guilty as Carol!

She stood beside Lucy's bed, listening to her relaxed breathing. She longed to hold her, to draw comfort from that small warm body — but she carefully refrained from waking her. Her throat tightened. How much longer, she wondered, before Lucy was no more to her than a bitter-sweet memory!

After a while the house became quiet. Everyone had gone to bed, and there was still no sign of Ian. Holly wandered along the passage to Bobby's room. His curtains were drawn back, and moonlight lit the room. He was lying on his back, one arm flung over his head. Cautiously she pulled the covers over him, and he murmured in his sleep and turned over. Holly touched his tousled hair, and then returned to her room.

She wished that Ian would come back, and yet dreaded the moment when he did. At last she made up her mind. She would place the envelope on his dressing-table, where he would see it when he returned. It would be easier that way. Picking it up, she went to his room.

The heavy velvet curtains were drawn. On a chair lay a pair of discarded trousers, and Ian's old tweed jacket. She ran her fingers across its roughness. Propping the envelope against the dressing-table mirror, she met her own reflection, large startled eyes in a face paler than usual, the soft full lips parted and vulnerable.

Holly shivered, and pulled the thin fabric of her *négligee* closer around her. She turned to leave, and her hand was already on the door handle, when it turned in her grip. Ian stood there, his tall frame looming above her, filling the doorway. He stepped inside.

'What the devil are *you* doing here?' His tone was quiet, and cold. His eyes burned under lowering brows. She took a step backwards. He advanced, shrugging off his jacket and letting it drop unheeded. His lips were in a harsh uncompromising line.

'Didn't you get my message? I never want to see you again.'

His eyes bored into hers, menace in their depths.

'Ian!' Her hand went out in supplication. 'I only went to get the proof I needed . . . we both needed. And I have it — it's there!'

Her words made no impression. He continued advancing, and she retreated before him until she felt the hard edge of the bed against her legs. She saw beads of perspiration on his forehead.

'I know only too well why you went. You couldn't keep away from him — could you! Even when I rang . . . what were you doing then? I'll see if she's dressed!' His sarcasm cut.

'No!' She put a hand against his chest, leaning away from him. 'No — Ian . . . it wasn't like that!'

His hands caught her by the shoulders. His fingers dug in to her flesh.

'This time — by God — you've driven me too far,' he snarled. 'This time you'll learn who you belong to!'

The next moment his arms were around her like bands of steel, his mouth on hers with brutal demanding passion. Her feet were swept from under her, and she found herself flung on the bed, his weight crushing her.

'No! No!' she tried to scream, but her breath had been forced from her lungs. His lips were on hers again, cruelly forcing them open, his tongue probing. With one hand he held her, and with the other he groped until his fingers clutched the delicate silk of her nightgown. Rolling away from her he tore downwards in one violent movement, and the flimsy material rent, revealing the firm warm whiteness of her body. Then more desperate movements, and she could feel him against her, covering her, body to body, skin against skin.

Holly struggled — her senses reeling. His hands were caressing her angrily, demanding a response — daring her to deny her own inner needs, and her breathing quickened as her own body began to betray her.

'No . . . please!' she moaned — but it was no use. She was swept down . . . down into a vortex, where an inexorable rhythm was sweeping her backward and forward, piercing her with an intensity that was unbearable. All sense of place and time was lost. All resistance melted under the onslaught of her own desire, and she clung to him with an abandon of which she was hardly aware. Helpless on a tide of sensation, she was driven to the edge of an abyss over which she plunged, crying his name over and over again, her body matching the rhythm of his, until she arched soundlessly against him — and then she heard the low agonized cry of his relief, and the vortex was filled with a sudden rush of molten gold.

After a long moment, Ian's weight

slid from her, but his head remained buried on her shoulder — his chest heaving in great shuddering breaths that might have been sobs. Holly's arms cradled him.

'Hush!' she whispered. 'I understand. Hush!'

She stayed like that, until sleep claimed both of them.

★　★　★

'Oh — my God!' Holly heard the strangled words, and struggled to consciousness. She remembered what had happened, with a spasm of grief and delight. Reluctantly she opened her eyes. It was morning. Ian was dressed, standing beside the dressing-table, his back to her.

'Ian?' Her voice was soft with remembered intimacy.

He spun round — and she saw the envelope in his hand. His face was white with shock — his eyes accusing. He thrust the papers towards her.

'Then it's true . . . it's true!'

The languorous warmth in her limbs drained away. 'Yes,' she replied stiffly. 'It's true. I'm not Carol — I'm her twin.'

A flood of red welled up, covering his neck and face. 'What have I done!' he breathed.

The sight of his shock — his denial — struck her like a blow. She made a desperate bid to gather up her tattered pride.

'It's not the end of the world,' she jibed. 'You're not my first, and I don't suppose you'll be the last!'

He looked at her dumbly. Let him believe it! she prayed. It will make it easier for him!

He seemed in a daze. 'I'm sorry . . . ' he broke off, and rushed from the room.

Back in her own bedroom, Holly dressed with the painful deliberation of a nightmare, hollow-eyed with self-recrimination.

You've always known you were only a

substitute! she told herself grimly. He never wanted you. He never has. It was his wife he held last night — not you. Never you!

The morning drew on, and the children claimed her.

'I knew you'd come back!' shouted Bobby, flinging himself at her.

Is there no end to the pain? she thought. She hugged them both. 'Yes, I came back — but it is nearly time for me to go for good. You must remember, we agreed I was only here for a little while!'

Lunchtime came, and still there was no sign of Ian.

'I don't like it,' said Flora, as they ate an uncomfortable meal. 'He might do something silly!'

'Don't talk daft, girl,' snapped her father. All the same, Holly saw his hands tremble as he lit up his pipe. She could stand no more of it.

'I'm going to find him,' she said.

'I'll come with you,' said Flora.

'No!' Holly gave her a look of appeal.

'I think it best if I go alone.'

Flora looked at her, and comprehension dawned. She put her arms around Holly.

'Oh, I wish it *had* been you!' she whispered.

★ ★ ★

Holly went out — not knowing where to look. There was a balmy feel to the air which gave a hint of the Spring to come, a keen smell of wet earth and hidden growth. She turned, and took the path to the plantation. It was muddy now, and slippery, but she soon gained the top.

From there the river looked wider than it had been, fed by the melting snows. A wild thought touched her mind, but she quelled it fiercely. No! That would not be Ian's way.

She turned to look the other way, remembering the first time she had come there with him. As she stood, the wind ruffling her curls, she ached for the remembered innocence of that day. Then she saw him, below her in a dip that was filled with heather. He was sitting on a boulder, his head in his hands.

She went bounding and sliding down the hillside towards him, and he looked up. For one wild hopeful moment she thought he was about to hold out his arms to her — but he stood still.

She slithered to a halt. 'You . . . you didn't come to lunch We were worried . . . ' Her voice tailed off.

'It was kind of you to bother. Tell Flora I'll be back.' He made it clear that he did not want her to accompany him. She flushed, and turned to go.

'Holly!'

She turned eagerly — but he was still withdrawn, distant — his eyes dark with self-loathing.

'It's futile for me to apologize. You did so much for us, and I kept you against your will. You are, of course, free to leave as soon as you wish.'

I don't ever want to leave you! The

cry was deep inside her, but she bit back the words. Her answer was just as formal as his.

'In the circumstances it might be as well.'

He rubbed the back of his hand across his eyes. 'I realize you've been here all this time without recompense. I shall, of course, put that right before you go . . . '

'No!' The blood rushed to her cheeks. 'I don't want payment!' Her bitterness and indignation welled up.

'Please! Don't make me feel any guiltier than I do!'

She bent her head. 'Very well,' she said in a low voice. She turned away. 'I'll tell Flora you are on your way.'

By the time she reached the house she had pulled herself together. 'It's all right,' she said with an attempt at a smile. 'He's on the hill, watching the deer — he'll be back soon.'

'I told you so!' said his father. 'Didn't I say so, Flora? You women make too much of things!'

Flora smiled, but Holly knew she was not deceived. 'There was a phone call for you,' she said. 'Doctor Sinclair has a woman willing to come, if we still want her. I said I'd ring back.'

Holly winced. She was being allowed no way out. 'You'd better tell him she can start tomorrow,' she said. 'I shall be leaving.'

The old man looked dismayed. 'No, lassie! There's no need! Everything will settle down.'

'It's no use,' said Holly gently. 'Ian would rather I went.'

'I'm sorry, Holly,' said Flora. 'I wish it could have been otherwise.'

'I'll go and start packing,' said Holly, awkwardly. The doorbell rang. 'I'll get it,' she said. When she opened the door Felix was standing there, looking incredibly unruffled.

'Well, Holly darling,' he drawled with an engaging grin. 'I thought I'd see for myself what it is that's so enticing about foreign parts.'

'Oh, Felix!' She flung her arms

around him, and hugged him tight. He was startled at her pallor, and the desperation in her eyes.

'Felix — take me away from here,' she cried. 'Please take me away!'

9

Having quickly recovered her poise, Holly took Felix into the house and introduced him. He was at his best, urbane and charming. Flora was completely won over. Although she had been so relieved to see him, Holly now was not so certain. He introduced another element into the situation, and she was not sure what that meant.

'It's very beautiful here,' said Felix, gazing out of the window in rapt admiration. 'I can well see why Holly is so fond of it!'

Old Mr. MacEwan was pleased. 'Aye — we pride ourselves on living in one of the most beautiful parts of Scotland.'

Felix — you crafty devil! thought Holly, knowing him to be incapable of appreciating anything beyond a fifty-mile radius of Hyde Park. She was impatient to see what he was up to.

After a while Flora rose. 'I expect you two will want to chat — and I must see to the children. They've been in the kitchen plaguing Maggie.'

Felix stood, politely. 'Come on, Father,' said Flora sharply. 'I have things for you to do!'

When they had gone Holly took the initiative. 'Felix! What on earth are you doing here? And don't tell me you were just passing by!'

He examined the furniture and ornaments, wincing occasionally. 'Heavy, my dear!' he murmured. 'Positively Gothic!'

'Felix — stop it,' she warned. '*Why* are you here?'

'My concern for you, my darling — plus a certain amount of curiosity. I wanted to see for myself what was going on. Don't forget, I spoke to that fellow over the phone. If ever a man was at the end of his tether, he was! I didn't like it. So, when old Beddowes offered to swap turns with me, I jumped at it.'

He put his hands on her shoulders. 'You should have listened to me, you silly little chump. These people are nothing to you — you shouldn't have got involved. However, I'm here now.'

There was a smug tone of masculine superiority in his voice, and a flash of annoyance shot through Holly.

'Felix — it was very kind of you. I do appreciate your concern,' she said softly. 'But you really needn't have bothered. As a matter of fact, I plan to return to London tomorrow.'

'Ha!' He pounced on the inference behind her words. 'So you've told your fiery Scot the news? How did he take it?'

Again a flash of irritation. 'As one would expect,' she said carefully.

Felix's green eyes were fixed on her face. He smiled. 'Good,' he said smoothly. 'And does he still want to find your sister?'

Holly's nerves felt ragged. I shall scream in a moment! she thought. 'Of course he does!' she flashed. 'She's still his wife, isn't she? Naturally he wants to find her!'

His air of triumph grew. Fishing in

his breast pocket he took out a slip of paper. Holly read it with a puzzled frown. She looked at him sharply.

'You don't mean . . . it can't be . . . '

'Oh yes it is!' he laughed. 'I'm not just a handsome face, you know. That's her address in Glasgow.'

'But I don't understand.' She was half reluctant to believe him. 'How could you trace her so quickly?'

'But my dear, I'm a genius!' he teased. 'I will admit that I had one vital bit of information — the letter you left with me. At the hotel I chatted up the girl on reception, and made an excuse to examine the register for that date. I was looking for a man on his own, with a first name Grant, or at least the initial G. It was easy enough. Well — what will you do? Give the address to Ian?'

'Of course,' said Holly slowly. 'But how do we know she is still there — she might have moved on.'

'I thought of that,' said Felix. 'I rang the number he had given on the register, and she answered. She sounded just like you — even to the slight London accent. Oh, it was Carol, there's no doubt in my mind.'

'What did you say to her?'

'I made some excuse about a wrong number. I didn't want to scare her off.' He gave Holly a probing glance. 'Now you can pass this on to her husband, and he can get his wife back again, and everyone will be happy!'

Holly sat staring at the piece of paper. She felt as though the room was closing in on her. She jumped to her feet and stood staring out of the window. Felix pressed home his advantage.

'Tomorrow I'll take you back to where you belong.'

She looked at him, dismayed. 'But Felix — Mrs. Barnes has given away my room. I've nowhere to go.'

He crossed to where she stood, and put his hands on her waist, smiling. 'Then you'll have to come home with me, my dear!'

Holly shook her head, decidedly. 'No

— really Felix. You are very kind, but I couldn't.'

'No strings attached, my sweet,' he insisted. 'I promise you. Just until you find a place of your own.'

Holly's objections died on her lips. Felix had left her no way out. He was determined to be her knight-errant, and she did not seem to have much choice. She gave a helpless shrug.

'Oh, very well, Felix, and thank you. I accept, but only until I sort things out.'

'Let's seal the bargain,' said Felix. Pulling her closer he kissed her lightly on the lips.

Afterwards Holly thought it inevitable that Ian should choose that moment to arrive. That was the way things happened to her! Felix did not release her at once. He tightened his grip, and kept one arm possessively around her. Ian's expression was inscrutable. He advanced upon them, hand outstretched to Felix.

'Flora told me of your arrival. You will of course stay here the night. I feel

I owe you a great apology. Twice I've been rude to you over the phone. I expect you realize I was under the impression that your fiancée was my wife.'

Felix's fiancée! Whatever gave him that idea? Holly opened her mouth to protest, but Felix gave her no chance.

'Yes — strange business that — eh? Still, all's well that ends well, isn't it, darling?'

Ian's eyes held hers, but she could not read the message in their depths. He was so far from her now — what did it matter any more what he believed? She was aware of Felix watching her. She held the paper out to Ian.

'Here's Carol's address. Felix discovered it.'

He took it from her. For a moment it seemed he was about to speak, but the moment passed. He turned instead to Felix.

'You're certain about this?'

'Absolutely!'

'Then I am very much in your debt.'

'Will you . . . when will you see her?' asked Holly.

He gave her a dark glance. Was it scorn she saw in his eyes? She could not tell.

'First thing in the morning.' He stopped, as a thought struck him. 'Of course, if you wish to see her . . . '

'Oh no!' said Holly, hurriedly. How could she bear to see him with Carol? Too much had come between her and the sister she had never known. It was too late to meet her now.

'I would rather you didn't mention me,' she said. 'I shall be going back to London with Felix in the morning.'

He acknowledged her words with a stiff nod. 'If I should need to get in touch with you at all . . . ?'

'She'll be at my address,' interrupted Felix smoothly.

Holly realized Felix was deliberately making their relationship appear more than it really was — but what did it matter, anyway? She could not be bothered to put things right. She felt drained of all initiative.

As they sat at dinner that evening, she kept looking at Ian, drinking in every detail of his face, aware of the passing minutes that brought her nearer to saying goodbye.

What was he thinking? she wondered. His manner to her was correct — distant even. Was he bitterly regretting his behaviour of the night before . . . was he consumed by feelings of guilt? Ever since they had first met, events had pushed them both inevitably towards this conclusion. She could not — would not — regret what had happened. She had belonged to him, surrendering all the love and understanding that had been growing in her, day by day, since first she had met him. And she was glad!

That night, she lay awake in the darkness, re-living the moments she had spent in this house. When sleep finally did claim her, it was filled with troubled dreams.

The next morning the goodbyes were

not easy to say. Lucy did not, in any case, really understand what was happening, and wriggled out of Holly's grasp, to run away and play.

'Goodbye, baby,' Holly whispered.

With Bobby it was worse, because she was aware of his efforts to appear grown-up and casual.

'I'll send you a postcard of Buckingham Palace,' she promised.

'Yes — 'cos I'd like that.' Then he flung his arms around her waist. 'I love you, Holly,' he blurted, and tore from the room, banging the door behind him.

Holly's heart was heavy as she picked up her overnight bag, and carried it into the hall. Felix was already outside, tinkering with the car. Maggie and Flora came to see her off, and Father too. As they embraced she wondered whether he would ever finish his book now.

'Make him keep at it!' she said to Flora. 'And you marry that Malcolm of yours.'

'I'll see what I can do,' said Flora, without indicating which remark she was answering.

'Thank you for a wonderful Christmas, Maggie. I shall never forget peeling those potatoes!'

'Stop feeling sorry for yourself!' said Maggie bluntly, eyes suspiciously bright. 'There'll be many good Christmasses for you yet.'

They came out to wave her goodbye. Ian was not with them. She thought bleakly that perhaps he had already left to find Carol, without sparing her a thought — but as she put her case into the boot of Felix's car, he came around the corner of the house. He had an envelope in his hand.

'You mustn't forget this,' he said. 'It's the wages I owe you. I want you to have it — no argument.'

His face became blurred, and she blinked hard, taking the envelope without really knowing what she was doing.

'I hope . . . I hope everything works

out for you,' she said.

'And for you . . . and Felix,' he replied.

Time hung painfully between them. Suddenly he pulled her to him, and she felt his lips brush her temple.

'Goodbye . . . Holly.'

She ran to the car. Felix had the door open, and the engine running. He tooted his horn as he drove away. Holly did not even look around.

★　★　★

For some time they drove in silence.

'Aren't you going to see what's in that envelope?' asked Felix.

She had forgotten that she was holding it. She stared at the cheque inside, scarcely registering the figure written there. Felix whistled.

'Not at all bad!'

She took a second look. 'I can't accept this,' she said dully. 'It's more than a year's salary!'

'Don't be a fool,' said Felix. 'He can

obviously afford it. Besides,' he added shrewdly, 'if you sent it back you'd only make him feel bad — you wouldn't want that now, would you?'

Holly shook her head. She was too emotional to speak.

'Here,' said Felix. He handed her a large handkerchief. 'I don't want people to think I've been beating you!'

It was only then that she realized that tears were running down her cheeks.

★ ★ ★

Three months later, Spring came to London, clothing the trees with mantles of delicate green, and brightening the parks with displays of tulips and daffodils.

Holly came up from the tube station, after a hard day's work, clutching a bag of groceries.

She crossed the busy road, dodging through the traffic, and turned down a quiet side street. It led to a railed garden area. She skirted this, looking up at the high shuttered houses that surrounded it. Anyone lucky enough to have a flat on the first or second floors would have a pleasant outlook across the trees but she would not be one of them.

She balanced the groceries on a dust bin, as she inserted the key into the lock of the basement flat of number twenty-three. At least, she had a home of her own, and for that she was truly grateful.

Inside, she dumped her things onto one of the armchairs. It was shabby, like the rest of the flat, but comfortable enough. She carried the groceries into the tiny kitchenette. She was still in a muddle, after moving in the previous day. Felix had helped, but there had not been time to unpack more than a few essentials.

Her new job in the old people's home was physically and mentally demanding. It was not that she really disliked her work — she was only too glad to have found a position at last!

She cut a slice of wholemeal bread, and whipped up a quick omelette. From the small and battered fridge she took the milk for her coffee. Then she carried it all on a tray into the living-room. Sinking into a chair, she balanced the tray on her lap.

As she ate, she looked around her critically. Cardboard boxes cluttered the floor, and although it was a bright day outside, she already needed the electric light. As yet, her surroundings were not very attractive — but flats were hard to come by, and it was only Ian's cheque that had enabled her to take on the lease of this one for a year.

Felix had been very critical. 'Holly — it's a dump!' he had exclaimed. 'Why on earth do you insist on coming here? We are perfectly comfortable as we are!'

But it had not been right for Holly to stay any longer in his flat — and they both knew it.

Her meal finished, she washed up the few dishes, and made a start on the boxes. She worked methodically — her expression withdrawn. She was thinner in the face than she had been, and there was a determined line to her mouth. As she worked, she thought of Felix's words.

'Damn it, Holly — I want to marry you. We get on so well together. Why not say yes?'

Once more she had refused him, fondly but firmly. At last he accused her.

'It's Ian MacEwan, isn't it? You're in love with him. You have been, right from the time you went up there!'

She had admitted it. It was bitter-sweet relief, to say it out aloud.

'Yes, Felix — I love Ian, and I know I always will. I'm sorry!'

He had tried hard to persuade her, using one argument after another. 'It's over, Holly — you must come to terms with it!'

At last she could stand no more.

'Felix!' she blurted. 'I *know* it's over. But please, please stop! There's something you don't know. I'm pregnant!

I'm going to have Ian's child.'

There was a long silence. Eventually, 'Does he know?' asked Felix.

Holly shook her head. 'So you see . . . ' she continued brightly, busying herself frantically, ' . . . I shall be far too busy looking after the baby, to take you on as well!'

He had come to her then, and held her tight. He was too honest to pretend that her news had not changed everything.

'Don't hesitate to call on me, if you need help,' he said.

'I shall be fine,' she had reassured him. 'I don't have a lot of stairs to climb, and I'll be able to sit out in the gardens, with the baby. Felix — I'll never forget what you've done for me . . . but I *want* Ian's child.'

Then he had left her. So — today — she was glad to be here alone. Felix would always be around as a friend, she knew. That was something to be grateful for.

Holly carried some of the empty

boxes, and put them outside the door for the dustmen to collect on their next visit. There was only one box to unpack now. She returned to it, and the very first thing she took from it was the carving Ian had given her.

She sat holding it, and desolation swept through her. She had tried so hard not to dwell on memories, but there was always something to remind her — the sudden laughter of a child, or the unexpected glimpse of someone who looked like Ian.

She could see him so clearly — those blue eyes, the brown unruly hair, the strong lines of his face. She often saw him so in her dreams, and felt his arms around her — but there had been no word from him since she had left — only a postcard from Bobby in answer to one of hers.

What had happened, she wondered? Was Carol back there with the family, or had Helen taken her place? Above all — was Ian happy?

She placed the carving carefully on

the sideboard. It was no use looking back, she realized that. She had to go forward, for his child's sake.

At first, when she had found out she was pregnant, she had been afraid. But now, she was glad. She would not see Ian again, but she had not lost him altogether.

She wandered back to the carving, and caressed the little faces with her fingers. Her child would never know those other children, who had come to mean so much to her. Would never run with them on the hills, and look down on that house, tucked safely below. The familiar ache returned. Oh Ian! He would never know just how much she needed him.

The doorbell rang, and she returned reluctantly to the present. Not Felix with more offers of help! she thought. She was not in the mood for company this evening. She opened the door with excuses at the ready.

'Can I come in?' asked Ian. Holly stared at him, speechless.

'Of . . . of course,' she stammered at last. She wanted to touch him, to reassure herself that it was not some hallucination — but she was afraid to, for fear that he might vanish! Certainly nothing could have been less like a phantom. He seemed to fill the room, taller and broader than ever.

She ran a distracted hand through her curls.

'Ian . . . how did you know my new address? I'm sorry . . . I'm not being very polite. Please sit down. Excuse the muddle, but I've only just moved here. I'll make a cup of coffee.'

She was aware that she was babbling — and when he caught hold of her hands, and forced her to look at him, she was powerless to resist. His eyes bored into hers.

'Felix rang me,' he said quietly. 'He put me right on quite a few things. Holly . . . why did you let me believe you were engaged to him?'

'I didn't!' she protested. A small smile touched the corners of her mouth. 'You jumped to conclusions. You are very good at that, Ian!'

He acknowledged her thrust, with a wry smile. 'But you seemed eager to leave with him. I thought . . . well, I thought that was what you wanted, and that the least I could do was to keep out of your life from then on.'

She looked away from him. 'Felix had no right to ring you,' she whispered. 'What did he tell you?'

'Everything!'

'Everything?' She looked back at him, her eyes troubled. He lifted his hand and stroked her hair, and then ran his fingers along the line of her jaw.

'Little firebrand! Why didn't you let me know? Why did you hide away and try to manage all on your own? Holly, come back and marry me.'

She caught her breath. 'But — what about Carol?'

He shook his head. 'That's over. It has been over for a long time. She doesn't ever want to come back. In fact she is planning to emigrate with Grant, once the divorce is through. I think she is glad that I found her — it finalized things. She told me that she had been trying to pluck up the courage to end our marriage for years. That was why she behaved as she did. She had some cock-eyed idea that if she was bad enough I would be glad to let her go.' His lips twisted wryly. 'She thought that if she gave me children, it would be a sort of recompense. She never considered them to be hers.'

'And Helen?' Holly's eyes searched his face. 'What about her?'

He wrinkled his brow in bewilderment. 'Helen? What has she to do with it?'

'You were with her,' said Holly. 'The night . . . the night I came back from London.'

He seemed amused. 'I went to pay her the back wages I owed her. After that, I spent the evening playing chess with Doctor Sinclair. You surely couldn't think . . . oh, you little goose!'

He took her in his arms. 'I was a fool

to let you go,' he murmured. 'Come back with me. The children need you — we all need you. We can be married, just as soon as the divorce is through.'

When she did not answer he held her at arm's length.

'You're not worried about the legal aspect, are you?' he asked. 'I've checked all that . . . it is quite in order. As for the family, they will be delighted.'

As she remained silent, he continued. 'You'll love it up there now, Holly. Spring has arrived. There are already some calves in the herd, and more to be born. You promised you would watch — you *must* come back.'

Her eyes were wistful, as she shook her head.

'Thank you, Ian,' she said. 'I'm very proud that you've asked me, but I can't.'

He stood, dumbfounded. Deliberately, he sat down on the sofa, and made her sit beside him.

'Let's take this slowly,' he said. 'I'm not going to make the mistake of misunderstanding again. Felix said you told him that you loved me.'

Holly lowered her eyes. 'I don't deny it.'

'And you are going to have my child?'

Oh Felix! she thought. You dear, helpful man — what have you done, damn you! Her cheeks flamed, but she looked up at him, and her gaze was steadfast.

'Yes — that's true.'

'Then why, for heaven's sake!' he exploded. 'What's wrong now?'

She longed, above all else, to be able to throw herself into his arms, but she could not. It was kind of him to come to her — no doubt his strong sense of responsibility had prompted him to do it — but she could not allow him to make a second mistake. It would be wrong to take advantage of him, just because he felt he owed her something.

'Ian,' she said gently. 'It wouldn't work. I would only ever be second best for you . . . just a substitute for Carol. You would always realize that, and it would never be quite enough for you. I don't think I could bear living with you, knowing it . . . I love you too much. There's no need to feel guilty about what happened — it was my fault as much as yours — I will be all right!'

His reaction was sudden and violent. She was in his arms, and his kisses rained down on her face, fast and furious, leaving her breathless.

'Does this feel like second best?' he demanded. 'Damn it, Holly . . . I don't want to marry you because I'm sorry for you . . . or even because of the baby! I'm not trying to make an honest woman out of you!'

He kissed her again, a long satisfying kiss. 'Don't you see, it was *you* I was in love with all along. *You* were all I was always looking for in Carol, and never found. She accused me of never seeing her as she really was — and she was right. When you came, it was like a miracle. For the first time I found what I really wanted, and I was desperate to keep it. I suppose, deep down, I realized you weren't my wife, but I refused to let myself believe it, because I was afraid of losing you. It's you that I want, Holly — always and only you!'

At last she recognized the truth in his eyes, and something inside her began to melt — a need that had been with her for the whole of her life.

As she slid her arms around his neck, her eyes were shining.

'If you put it like that,' she murmured, 'how can I refuse? What are you waiting for, Ian MacEwan, my love. You had better help me to repack all these boxes. And then,' she added between breathless little kisses, ' . . . you can take me home. Take me home . . . to my family!'

We do hope that you have enjoyed reading this large print book.

Did you know that all of our titles are available for purchase?

We publish a wide range of high quality large print books including:
Romances, Mysteries, Classics
General Fiction
Non Fiction and Westerns

Special interest titles available in large print are:
The Little Oxford Dictionary
Music Book, Song Book
Hymn Book, Service Book

Also available from us courtesy of Oxford University Press:
Young Readers' Dictionary
(large print edition)
Young Readers' Thesaurus
(large print edition)

For further information or a free brochure, please contact us at:
Ulverscroft Large Print Books Ltd.,
The Green, Bradgate Road, Anstey,
Leicester, LE7 7FU, England.
Tel: (00 44) 0116 236 4325
Fax: (00 44) 0116 234 0205

A HEART DIVIDED

Karen Abbott

During World War Two, the German occupation of Ile D'Oleron, off the west coast of France, brings fear and hardship to the islanders. As the underground freedom-fighters strive to liberate their beloved island, Florentine Devreux finds her heart torn between two brothers. But it seems she has fallen in love with the wrong one! The events following the Normandy landings force her to think again — but has her change of heart come too late?

SHADOW OF THE FLAME

Sheila Belshaw

When zoology student Lisa Ryding first meets wildlife film-maker Guy Barrington at Oxford University, she is prepared to follow him to the ends of the earth. But a secret too tragic for Guy to reveal makes this impossible. Five years later, they are thrown together on a remote game reserve in Zambia by their mutual passion to save the elephant from extinction. When Guy is bitten by a snake and nearly dies, Lisa realises that nothing will ever change her love for him and her only salvation will be to never see him again.

ECHOES OF YESTERDAY

Rachael Croft

Vet Keira Forrest thought she'd seen the last of GP Daniel Grant after he callously dumped her best friend, but now she finds herself having to give him emergency first aid after an accident. Worse, her new job is right next door to his surgery and the local matchmakers are busy. She is determined to avoid him, but an engaging wolfhound puppy named Finn and a family of delinquent cats have other ideas.